Morbid Tales

By Devon L. Miller

Edited by Reggie Lutz
Cover art by Janell R. Colburn

To Skyla & Elaina,
Hope you enjoy!
Best Wishes,

Disclaimer: Herein lie works of fiction. Any resemblance to persons, living or dead, and events is coincidental.

ISBN: 1517314860
ISBN-13: 978-1517314866

DEDICATION

This book is dedicated to all those who never got to spend the night in the creepy old house at the end of the lane.

CONTENTS

ACKNOWLEDGMENTS

When a book has been over a decade in the making, there are quite a few people who need to be thanked. There have been many over the years who have supported me in my journey as a writer and helped—even in the smallest ways—bring this book into the world. You all deserve a huge thanks.

Thank you to my amazing family. To Becky and Howard Miller (a.k.a. Mom and Dad), for allowing me to be me, and not pushing me in some sensible direction like business management or accounting. To my husband, Joe, for being my biggest cheerleader and metaphorical ass-kicker. (How often those jobs are one in the same!) "Angel of Mercy" would not have happened without you. To my parents-in-law, Janice and Taras Merza, for embracing me (and my work), with love and support. Also, many thanks to the army of supporters made up of siblings, cousins, aunts, uncles, and chosen family. This writing life is so much easier because of you.

Thank you to the beta readers: Rachel Schmidt, Ronald Lyncha, and Reggie Lutz. You guys rock! Reggie, not only did you provide invaluable feedback, but then you further enlisted your red pen to be my editor. You are a great friend, supporter, and creative partner. Hugs and high-fives! Thanks also to Janell R. Colburn for cover art that makes my little dark heart sing.

And of course, thank you, dear reader.

INTRODUCTION

Love Sonnet for the Monsters

When dark descends the mighty werewolves howl
And specters float from their crypts in the night.
Take care and listen for the demon's growl
As vampires perform an ancient blood rite.
One dare not step into the mummy's tomb,
And should not walk on zombies' vacant graves.
For these things surely can mean a man's doom,
No solace found at the mouths of bats' caves.
A letter in blood sent by raven's claw,
Received with shaking hands and bated breath,
Only to be snatched by the hellhound's jaw,
Or the cold grip of the one we call Death.
To some, a terrible nightmare it seems,
To me, it makes for most romantic dreams.

-DLM

The Stretch

"GPS signal lost," the digitized female voice repeated for the tenth time that minute.

"No shit, Sherlock," Lyla replied. Like the GPS signal, she was lost. "That's what I get for trying to get around an accident."

She pulled off the road and turned on her flashers. Flipping on the internal lights, she reached for the road atlas she kept on the seat next to her. She could read a map, a skill for which she had not patted herself on the back until she realized how many people could not, having lost the skill in their dependence on technology. While it was technology that alerted her to the accident and advised her to take the next exit, it seemed it would not be technology to get her back on track again.

She traced her finger over the lines on the page, looking for her location in relation to the interstate. "Wait. What the…" she muttered to herself. She couldn't find the section of interstate she had been on anywhere on the map. "Damn it," she spat as she considered how outdated her atlas might be. It had been a gift when she turned 16 and got her license. It was inscribed, "The world is open to you now. May you always know your way. Love, Mom." The sentiment attached was the reason that she'd never replaced the atlas, though she'd owned three different cars since then. After all, how often could roads change?

She plucked her phone from its perch on the dash and stared at it as if she could will it to find the signal. She'd never been in a zone this dead and suspected that there was something wrong with her navigation application. "Fuck it," she said. Having less patience for troubleshooting than she did for driving, she tossed her phone onto the seat next to her and put her car back in gear.

Getting back on track again could be as simple as stopping to ask for directions and a road map, though she tried not to think of how much further she might have to drive before she found a place to do so. Convenience stores on the rural Pennsylvania road were few and far between, and most were closed this late. Lyla checked the time. At just after four in the morning, she guessed that the next gas station would be closed too. This was not a problem she'd have encountered on the interstate or any place close to it. She swallowed her anxiety and pressed the gas pedal harder.

Getting pulled over wouldn't necessarily be a bad thing.

In an effort to quell her anxiety, Lyla turned on the radio. The voice of a deejay between songs made her feel less alone, less lost. She hit the seek button and waited until she heard something promising. She glanced away from the road to stop the radio on Bon Jovi's "Livin' on a Prayer" and almost didn't see the glowing eyes in the headlights. She slammed on the breaks, narrowly missing the white tail bounding off into the woods. A road sign, a yellow diamond with a silhouette of a deer, glowed its "I-told-you-so" from the shoulder.

"Thanks for the warning," she muttered. "And thank *you* for stopping on a dime," she said as she patted the dashboard of her Chrysler 300. "You're such a good car, Samantha." She meant it. To her, the powerful engine and tough, American body in gun-metal gray provided peace of mind, the confidence that in the event of an accident she couldn't outmaneuver, she stood a chance of walking away. She just hadn't intended on testing her theory on the North American white tail deer. "At least I'm awake now."

She was tired. There was no question about that. It was why she didn't want to lose time waiting for an accident to clear. Now she feared how far off track she'd gotten and how much more time it might cost her. She couldn't even be sure of where she was. The warning sign for deer was one of the first signs she'd seen a while, which didn't make sense. She reasoned that she'd been missing signs in her tiredness and resolved to stay alert, hoping she might see a sign pointing her toward the interstate.

With every field and wooded area she passed, her anxiety grew. She'd driven for miles and hadn't seen so much as a speed limit sign. Lyla imagined that people who lived in an area this rural did so for the open space and clean air, but the feeling of being trapped in a valley that wasn't showing her a way out inhibited her breathing. She imagined the mountains closing in on her in the darkness as she drove into another heavily wooded area.

The trees badly needed to be trimmed. Branches reached for the car with skeletal fingers that bore only the lightest wisps of leaves so early in the year. Though the foliage was sparse, the road ahead loomed like a dark tunnel. Lyla had been warned about the condition of Pennsylvania roads but never dreamed they would appear this ominous. She groaned at a cliché joke about Ozzy Osbourne and a bat head when something heavy and black swooped in front of her car. "What the hell!" she exclaimed as she swerved to miss something that she could no longer see. She slowed down, her eyes wide but seeing nothing.

Believing her eyes were playing tricks on her, Lyla thought it was time to find a safe place to pull over. If simple shadows were becoming hallucinations, she was far too tired to be operating a vehicle.

"It's just shadows," she said. "Only shadows," she kept repeating to herself as she scanned the roadside for a pull-off.

Had she not seen the sign for the snow plow turnaround, she would have missed the pull off completely. She skidded off the road and fishtailed in the gravel before coming to a stop.

"*This* sign you have," she muttered though she was grateful for it. Given the warm, early spring night, she figured a snow plow turnaround was as good a place as any to pull over. She shut off the engine and double checked to make sure the doors were locked before reclining in the driver's seat. It wouldn't hurt to take a nap. In a couple of hours she could be certain that even the most rural convenience stores and gas stations would be open in the bright light of morning. It would be much better to try and get back on track then. She set the alarm on her phone—still no signal—and closed her eyes.

Lyla jolted awake to the sound of a screeching howl. She thought she'd dreamed the noise until she heard it a second time. She thought back to her time in Girl Scouts, to the forestry unit in junior high Biology, to her first real camping trip as an adult and she could think of nothing that made that sound. She wondered what poor creature was being killed when she heard it again, only much closer.

She sat alert, willing herself to spontaneously acquire night vision. She tried to focus on the trees to her right when she heard scratching to her left. She whipped her head in the direction of the sound but saw nothing.

The handle on the rear passenger side door jiggled as the howl came again. It sounded like it was just behind her on the driver's side. Lyla turned the keys in the ignition and pulled back onto the road with a bigger spray of gravel than when she pulled in.

A string of curses flew from her mouth before she thought to control her breathing. It was the radio deejay's voice that eventually calmed her. The world was still out there and it was as normal as it ever was. Maybe she'd been disoriented upon waking and misinterpreted what she heard.

The first hint of static edged its way onto the radio. "No!" she exclaimed. The deejay promised Meatloaf and his music always put Lyla in a better mood. The static came on faster than she would have suspected and she hit the seek button again. She needed the radio.

Sound sputtered through the speakers as the seek function searched for a station, but there was nothing but the faintest hint of words lost in static. Nothing came through for Lyla to choose. The last word she heard before giving up and shutting off the radio was "alone" as sung by Heart through static.

"Fuck," she said as she ripped a hand through her hair and rolled down the window. She needed air, but in spite of the freshness of spring, the smell filled her with dread. She thought back to every bit of safety advice she'd ever heard that amounted to, "Do NOT get out of the car," and couldn't help but apply it to the open window. "C'mon, c'mon," she urged the automatic window to close faster.

Lyla's chest rose and fell in shallow breaths as she fought to control them and the car. "What is going on?" she pleaded as shadows began diving around her Chrysler. Real or not, she couldn't deny that she saw them. She jerked the wheel and then overcorrected before deciding that nothing corporeal tries to be run over by a car. She concentrated on the lines on the road and gripped the wheel.

"We've been through worse, right, Sam," she spoke to her car, giving it the pep talk Lyla herself needed. "Remember Snow-mageddon? You rocked that and you're rear wheel drive. We got this," she said as she patted the dash and plowed through the gauntlet of phantoms, their sharp shadows clicking and scraping along the Chrysler's body but failing to slow it down.

Empowered by the confidence her car's performance gave her, she almost didn't notice the blackness coming up on her in the rearview mirror. It wasn't until the phantoms fell back, suspiciously receding, that Lyla thought to look behind her.

It started as pinhole, something she had to squint to be sure was there, but once she saw it, she could see that it was growing, rather, gaining on her.

A very real darkness chased her and she could not escape the feeling that if it caught her it would swallow her. It would relish in turning her car, her beloved vessel of freedom, into a tomb.

A red glow broke through a crack in the clouds above like someone had taken a giant scythe and slashed the sky's torso. Blood red light reflected in the hood of Lyla's car like a harbinger of death.

She pushed the pedal to the floor, hearing and feeling the engine roar as the needle on the speedometer rose. Though her friends and family joked about her lead foot, she would never have gone this fast on the interstate, much less a rural highway. The needle passed 105 miles per hour. Lyla's eyes flicked from the road ahead, to the needle, to the blackness behind her. The faster she drove, the faster it gained. The needle passed 115.

She knew that at some point the speed limiter would kick in and cut her acceleration, but it didn't matter. The road wasn't designed for this kind of speed, and there was a curve ahead.

Lyla no longer assumed she was imaging anything. The darkness laughed at her and she knew why. The darkness *might* kill her, but the accident she was setting herself up for most certainly would.

She pulled her foot off the pedal and whispered goodbyes to people who couldn't hear her.

The darkness gained and swirled up beside her. Swirls materialized into grotesques that grinned at her with malice. "Let's do this," she said as she flipped off a particularly sinister phantom skull snapping at her window. Then, instead of slamming the gas and racing again, she relaxed into her seat and guided her car around the bend.

The car began to shake and sputter as the inky blackness opened its formless mouth like a hungry shark. Lyla prepared herself for an unknown hell, but as she rounded the bend, shoulders tight and bracing for whatever was about to come, the morning sun peeked between the mountain and the clouds, illuminating the valley with a golden bright light that burned away the darkness. She heard a hiss as the monsters that dwelled there dematerialized into dust, giving way to the sparkle of morning dew.

As an added stroke of salvation, the road around the bend revealed a sign pointing toward the interstate. Lyla followed the direction and saw the illuminated neon lights of a gas station, the morning sun glinting on the overpass guard rail behind it. Nothing ever sparkled so brightly.

She pulled in and parked. Resting her head on the steering wheel, she thought of everything she'd just been through as she tried to catch her breath. Ultimately she decided, for the sake of her own sanity, not to examine the events too deeply. She'd heard horror stories and urban legends about haunted highways and she'd always chalked them up to grueling schedules imposed on exhausted truck drivers. It was an issue for labor unions to fight rather than paranormal investigators. She considered her experience on the road similar and vowed to be a better boss to herself, to never be that tired and lost and keep driving again. To keep her vow, she needed coffee and a new road atlas, just in case.

Minutes later, she exited the gas station, stopped in her tracks, and spilled the scalding hot coffee she carried down her front as she dropped the cup. Too shocked to feel it burn, she never registered that she'd spilled as she looked at her car.

Deep scratches ran from hood to trunk, and as she approached, she could make out prints in the dust by the handles in the doors that looked like claws.

Hungry Like the Wolf

Amber walked down the wooded path with him as he stumbled, the smell of alcohol on his breath. Darkness settled in slowly. She had begged Jim to take her home, but he was in no condition to drive. "No matter," she said with a shrug and a toss of her long, black tresses. It wasn't that far into town, so she said that she would walk. He insisted on coming along. Her honor needed to be protected, after all. It occurred to her that protecting her honor was the last thing on his mind. She didn't like him when he was like this, and the thought that her situation would be a safer one if she was by herself ran through her head as the hairs on the back of her neck stood on end and froze that way.

Her friends warned her not to go out with him that evening. They told her that she didn't know what she was getting into, but she dismissed their concerns. She had looked forward to the harvest party all summer, and no force in the heavens was going to stop her from going. *I'm in control of the situation*, she told herself and truly believed it.

14

If things started getting uncomfortable, she would leave.

But now she began to rethink all of her choices. Her discomfort grew as her legs itched with the need to run. It had rained earlier that day, and the mist crept up from the ground. *Sonofabitch!* She thought to herself as his hand—which had only moments before, while still at the party, been protectively resting on her shoulder—slid down to cup her breast. *This is the way scenes in bad horror movies start.* Bad horror movies weren't always wrong. She moved his hand away. This was no time for too much liquor, raging hormones, and desire to mix.

He moved his hand back and she pulled away from his grasp. "Come on, Jim. I told you, not tonight. I want to go home."

Jim still clasped a bottle of whiskey. He clumsily brought it to his lips and took a bigger drink than necessary. "So that's why you decided to go slinking down the path by yourself. No, you didn't want me to follow you at all," he said, his voice thick with sarcastic frustration as he tore a hand through his shaggy, blond hair.

Her eyes flashed in the dark. "I'm walking because you continued to get drunk and couldn't take me home! There's no sense in anyone getting killed—" She was cut off by a hard kiss on the mouth. When she shoved him away, she noticed that in his aggression, he had split her lip. She licked it and tasted blood.

He tasted it too. "Baby, I'm sorry," he said, and it seemed for a moment that she'd be free. No such luck. "But we both know you can handle a little pain, right?" he continued. She could tell that he wasn't through with these advances and they were alone.

This can't happen, she thought. *He has to let me go.* She had always been so comfortable in the woods, even at night. But she knew if this happened, the trees would know. They'd see, and her place of solace would become her place of shame.

He moved toward her and knocked her backwards. She winced against the impact as her head hit the ground hard.

"No!" she cried as he settled himself on top of her.

"I don't fuckin' get you, Amber!" he said, his voice rough and hoarse. He pinned her shoulders down and kissed her neck in a way that was more a bite than a kiss. "One minute we're hot and heavy and the next you're acting like some shy virgin!" He pulled his shirt over his head. "We both know that virgin shit isn't true. Now come on; let me feel those nails down my back again."

My God! He's going to get his way, she thought as she cried against the agony of splitting flesh as her nails extended into claws.

Then the clouds parted, and she saw the full moon in all its glory. She looked into eyes that were growing wide with shock and fear. "I begged you to take me home!" she sobbed, but the words came in growls and the tears were lost in the sleek, black fur growing on her face.

This time, the blood she licked from her lips was his.

Dream House

The faded Victorian mansion rose into the sky behind a wrought iron gate, crowded and half hidden by the overgrown rose bushes. Ivy, wild and out of control, choked the rose bushes in turn. Imposing oak trees cast dark shadows on the porch and their gnarled branches scraped against the windows.

I was thrilled when the real estate agent admitted to me that the reason the house was so inexpensive and had been available for so long was that the locals whispered that it was haunted. No one wanted to buy it at its true market value, if at all.

The front door groaned on rusty hinges and the shutters banged in even a light breeze. I was told that somewhere on the property was an old family cemetery, but since there hadn't been a groundskeeper in years, it was probably as overgrown as everything else. Finding it would require careful exploration. Sane people called the property a nightmare. I called it perfect and couldn't allow it to crumble to ruin.

When I was growing up, there was a house in my neighborhood that sat tucked away at the end of a long weather-beaten lane. It was the house in which kids dared each other to stay the night. No one was ever able. It had only remained standing because people were just as reluctant to tear it down as they were to live in it.

Twice I was supposed to spend the night in the house at the end of the lane, and twice my hopes were dashed.

The first time, I was twelve years old. My friends and I worked it out that we would be able to stay there while telling our parents we were going to be at each other's houses. It wasn't until the final Friday of the school year that the monkey wrench got thrown into the plan.

Somehow, by afternoon recess, our friend Kara found out what we were going to do and that we hadn't invited her. It wasn't so much that Kara was a snitch as it was that she was a chicken. We knew she wouldn't be able to spend the night in the spooky old house, and so we'd spent the week changing the subject when she walked by. We passed our notes when she couldn't see. We pulled off a number of shifty-eyed, sleight-of-hand communications. We were so close to having it all go off without a hitch, but then there we were, sitting on the merry-go-round when she ran up to us, red-faced, eyes puffy from crying. "I can't believe you guys would plan a party without me!"

We told her a gentler version of the truth. "We wanted to invite you, but we thought you'd be too afraid to go. We didn't think you'd have any fun."

She begged for us to take her. She swore that she could handle it and that she wouldn't be afraid. We all knew better. Of course, we also knew that she would keep on crying— quite possibly to any adult who would listen—if we didn't tell her she could come.

That night at about 10:00, Kara, looking every bit as distraught as she had on the playground, insisted that she needed to go home and that someone had to walk with her because it was dark and she was scared. I drew the short straw and headed out into the night with her.

I'm not sure how the whole thing played out after I left Kara at her doorstep, but by the time I got back to the creepy old house at the end of the lane, all of the rest of our parents were there, angry and exclaiming, "Just wait until we get home!" We spent the first two weeks of summer vacation grounded.

Kara spent the entire summer at her grandmother's, and the rest of us were too angry at her to think that anything but the best.

It was a couple of years before I got a second chance. A different group of us planned to stay in the house on the night of high school graduation, one last hurrah before going off to college. Unfortunately, the events of prom night ended that.

It seemed everyone who didn't have a curfew was doing something after the prom. Some people rented rooms at the hotel that was hosting it that year; others were simply going to take their cars up to the lookout, but most people were planning to at least stop by the "secret" party at the house at the end of the lane.

Most people, but not me. My curfew wouldn't be lifted until the night of graduation a couple of weeks later.

I wasn't there, so I didn't see the upstairs bedroom and its contents (including the captain of the football team and the homecoming queen in the throes of passion), crash through the dining room ceiling. I didn't hear the long, strained creak come from the floor of the dining room right before it, too, gave way and ended up in the basement.

Any time people die in an accident, it's a tragedy. When those people are pretty though, it's a tragedy upon which people take action. This one claimed the lives of five young, beautiful citizens with their whole lives ahead of them and injured quite a few more. It was the tragedy to end all tragedies in my town. In less time than it took to blink, police tape marked the perimeter of the house, the driveway gated, locked, and guarded. I don't know when exactly they tore the house down, but it was gone when I came home from college that Thanksgiving.

The house I had just purchased wouldn't meet that fate. It was mine and I wouldn't let it be condemned or torn down. I couldn't wait to get started on the renovations. I'd heard once that nothing stirred paranormal activity like home improvement projects. Only now it would be stirred in my very own haunted house, a house in which I would spend many more nights than one.

Everyone warned me that living in a home while making improvements could be stressful. I smiled and nodded through their unsolicited advice. My contractor had already tried to talk me out of it, citing all the work, some structural, which needed to be done. "In all honesty, I can't guarantee your safety living here during the renovation," he said, but his rhetoric did not dissuade me. I didn't want to miss a second of possible paranormal activity, and if the sleepless night was due to stress rather than a haunting, there was always something I could do to while away the hours. Banisters needed to be sanded and wallpaper needed to be stripped in addition to a number of other tasks I could do on my own.

I tucked myself into bed on my first night in the house dreaming of the ghostly possibilities. Was the creaking noise coming from the attic the ghost of the original owner's granny still rocking back and forth in her chair? Was the thumping sound the spirit of a heartbroken girl wandering the halls longing for her love to return? I was certain that as I continued my unpacking and really got into renovations to the property, the ghosts would make themselves known. I drifted off, letting the sounds of the creaky old house lull me to sleep. I couldn't have been happier.

The deeper I got into renovation the more that happiness faded as it became evident that the creaking and thumping were not caused by the paranormal but rather by the fact that the place was falling apart. Each problem fixed revealed another issue. Everything from the wiring and plumbing to the structure itself needed to be brought up to code. I even camped in my front yard for two weeks while workers installed new support beams to keep my home from crumbling on top of me. There were no restless spirits in the yard either.

Late one sleepless night I stood on the staircase scraping paper from the wall. My shoulders ached and I seriously considered just layering more paper on top of the existing mess rather than continuing on. It seemed I was finally getting tired. I climbed three steps higher than where I was working, where I'd left the bottle of merlot and a glass. I plopped down on the steps and poured. As I looked down into what would be my living room—once the ladders, tools, and table saws served their purposes and were removed—I sighed happily. Haunted or not, it was still going to be a really cool house once I finished bringing it back from the dead.

I sipped my wine and savored the moment down to each sore muscle. I'll never forget that feeling. I wish I had savored it longer.

I stood up and got a head rush. It should have been nothing, and had the loose banister not given way when I reached for it to steady myself, it would have been nothing. But the banister did give way and gravity did the rest.

People say that moments like these happen fast, but then, those are the people who survive. It started out fast, time moving too quickly for me to reach for something solid, too quickly to do anything but accept that I was going to fall. It shouldn't have been a bad fall, but the table saw lay in wait below. The instant I glimpsed it, time slowed down. I might as well have been waiting for a feather to fall on that blade, but my body was not a feather.

Of course, when I saw the blade sticking through the right half of my gut, a moment of panic that I was going to die before seeing my project to fruition gripped me. I thought about how this was all so unfair as my short life played itself back to me, but then there was peace. I wanted a haunted house, after all. I'd get it, even if I had to be the ghost.

I never expected my death in my home to rank among the prom night deaths of the kids I'd gone to high school with. It was really just a home renovation accident resulting in the death of a full-grown adult woman, and I was pleased that my house wasn't going to be torn down because of it. Nevertheless, it stung a little bit when my real estate agent started showing it to people again. Once, a woman asked the agent that had once been mine why the renovation stopped so abruptly. When my agent responded that she didn't know for sure and trailed off on some bank nonsense, I got so furious that I stomped off to my bedroom and slammed the door in a huff. The client did not purchase my house.

After a couple of tantrums like that, it occurred to me that if I couldn't control my temper, no one would buy my home and it would meet the very fate from which I'd tried to save it.

One day, as I was sitting on the stairs, not at all

surprised that I felt especially connected to them, I heard the voice of my realtor and another female voice that sounded oddly familiar. A male voice entered the conversation, but it was that second female voice that piqued my attention. I drifted down the stairs to get a better view of the entryway.

I couldn't believe it. Kara stood in my foyer, exclaiming how perfect it was to a man that I assumed was her husband. Then she went on to talk about the house at the end of the lane, the very same one from our childhood, laughing at how afraid she used to be of these beautiful old homes.

"Well, if you want," her husband said, "it can be our dream house."

"I want," Kara replied with a pouty-lipped smile.

My real estate agent's face beamed as my ethereal heart dropped. This really was entirely too unfair.

I know I should be happy that my home has been purchased, that the renovation will be completed, but I'll tell you this much: if I don't like Kara's design choices, I'll see her red-faced, eyes puffy from crying again, and for very good reason.

Exposure Therapy

My parents told me I was going for treatment the day after I turned seventeen. They presented it to me as though it was a good thing, one of my presents, and yet they didn't tell me until the day after my birthday.

"Are you serious?" I asked. I couldn't believe what I saw on the brochure in front of me. "An appreciation for horror flicks is a crime so egregious that I need to be shipped off to a treatment facility?" I did my best to remain calm. My parents had no patience for emotional responses.

"It's not a crime, honey," my mother said.

"It's an illness. It's sick to enjoy watching people getting slaughtered, even in fiction," my father said. "And we've ignored it for too long. You're seventeen, Mara, and will need to function as a productive, healthy member of society before you know it."

"And you just can't do that if you are so desensitized to violence and death that you've lost capacity for empathy," my mother said. A tear welled up in her eye and then disappeared again, like she'd pulled it back.

My parents' words were not their own. I'd heard them before. They were the words of Connor Wentworth, head of the lobbyist group A Health and Morality Focused Future. Their agenda was censorship and telling people how they should think. The horror movie industry had been one of Wentworth's crusades since 2042, when the story of a child who murdered his friends while trying to re-enact a film he'd seen got national attention. Wentworth went to work spreading the fear that any kid who took in a horror double feature was a killer in the making. Thankfully, the majority of people could see the flaw in his logic and the group had been largely unsuccessful in its lobbying. Even so, I knew that if I did some digging, I'd find Connor Wentworth's name attached to the Sunrise Treatment Facility, dedicated to instilling pure thought and behavior in the future of America since 2045, touted on the brochure in front of me. He could say whatever he wanted about the horror genre, but I'd never seen anything more chilling than the pristine whiteness of the building nestled between the too-green grass of the manicured lawn and the bright azure sky. Even the trees in the surrounding forest seemed oddly symmetrical, like the forest, too, might be landscaped. Nothing that clean and crisp existed without covering for something sinister.

I'd always thought my parents were too smart to fall for the Wentworth brand of fear-based crap. Upon finding out that they weren't, I fought the desire to scream and maintained my even tone. "I am not desensitized to real suffering and the fact that you want to send me away like this over my preference in fiction shows me that you are the ones who lack empathy." *Not to mention intelligence*, but that went unsaid.

"I'm done here," my father said and pushed himself away from the kitchen table, the place where all important family discussions were held. "The facility car will be here for you in an hour. I suggest you pack."

"An hour!" I called after my father who was already halfway down the hall. He considered the discussion finished, so it was, but I kept speaking in spite of the futility. "How long am I staying? What should I pack?"

My mother patted my hand, turning my attention back to her. "We signed you up for three weeks of treatment. You'll still have plenty of your summer left when you return home, and you'll be free to enjoy your senior year like a normal teenager."

"Have you talked to any normal teenagers recently?" I asked. I thought I'd made it fairly clear that I found "normal" teenagers insipid. Perhaps my candor was the problem.

In my mother's standard fashion, she ignored what she didn't want to hear and rolled over it. "And look, this place actually looks sort of cool." She pointed to a paragraph in the pamphlet. "They use virtual reality as part of treatment. It sounds like they can put you in the middle of one of these films you love as a tool to reconnect you with your sense of empathy."

That got my attention. As a technology geek in addition to a horror genre aficionado, I reasoned that this experience could be awesome, indeed, if not for the reasons intended. It was why I stopped fighting and packed as I was told. When the facility's self-driving car arrived, I got in, careful not to look back. I really hoped that little jab stung my mother as the television screen in the car came to life, auto-playing an orientation video once the car reached the designated speed. It wasn't until the car doors auto-locked me inside with Connor Wentworth's self-righteous smile on the screen that the bile rose up my throat. He was speaking with a Dr. Albert Hill, Director of Sunrise Treatment Facility, about what essentially boiled down to attempts at personality re-assignment.

I was calmed in the intake and waiting room, not by a needle full of sedatives as I'd feared, but by the smiling face of another patient.

"Aren't you freaking out?" I asked the boy who was about my age. He had shaggy brown hair, glasses, and a charming grin.

"Are you kidding? I've been dying to sign up for this program since I read about its development."

"Really?" I asked and raised my brow as I scanned the nervous faces of the other adolescents around the room.

"Really. Think about it. They get a bunch of crazed horror fans," he said as he wiggled his fingers and crooked them in a classic monster pose, "and lock us all together in a facility where they put us in virtual reality horror situations as some twisted, experimental form of exposure therapy. I mean, what did they really think they were going to accomplish but giving us all a bit of a thrill that we can go full horror geek about in the cafeteria?"

Well, since he put it that way. "I'm Mara," I said and offered my hand.

An intake assistant came through the door and called, "Michael Ferra!"

"Mikey," he corrected, but only to me as he shook my hand. "Catch you at the cool table," he said with a wink and then followed the intake assistant through the door.

Mikey's words proved to be less comforting without his

smile. His question pulsed like a neon sign in my head. What *did* they really think they were going to accomplish? The question made me shiver and I considered running, but then my name was called.

I suffered through the expected intake tedium: a standard physical, a scripted mental health screening, and a drug test before I was shown my room. The results were analyzed and I was cleared for the treatment.

My heart raced with anticipation as the good doctors hooked me up to their state-of-the-art virtual reality and slid the visor over my eyes. Instantly, I was transported into the horror world they intended to show me. A thick layer of grime covered a sepia toned room, and a thumping noise came from behind a doorway with light flickering through the cracks. I imagined a fictional person in a fictional audience whispering, "Girl, don't go in there," as I stepped toward the door, my hand reaching for the knob.

When I crept through, the smell hit me first: blood and so much meat, unmistakable though I'd never actually smelled it before. I thought virtual reality was supposed to appeal mostly to the sense of sight, but the smell of death and that thumping sound made my reality more actual than virtual.

Then I saw the body. The shell of what had probably

once been an attractive, well-muscled male hung from the ceiling by meat hooks in his shoulders, everything that was once the life inside him reduced to sticky gore dripping down his outside and congealing in a pool on the filthy tile floor beneath his dangling feet.

I forced myself to look at his face. It was frozen in wide-eyed terror, his mouth set in a soundless, perpetual scream. Past the body, a curtain hung from the ceiling. The light behind it cast a silhouette of a large figure. Over and over, the figure raised its arm, meat cleaver in hand, and dropped it onto what could only be another corpse laid out on a heavy table. Each time the arm came down, thick liquid splashed against the curtain. I clapped a hand over my mouth to stifle my own scream. I didn't want to alert the source of the thumping sound that I was there.

This was too real and I had lost my nerve. I turned to leave the way I had come, but the door was gone. Trapped with at least two corpses and a madman, I pinched my eyes shut and waited for the horror ride to be over. "It's not real. It's not real," I repeated in whispers to myself.

"Oh it's not?" a voice grunted close to my face.

I opened my eyes to rotten teeth inside a stinking mouth on a lacerated face. The man—if you could call him a man— was so foul and deformed that I was willing to bet he was some sort of demon from Hell.

He grabbed my arm, his grimy, misshapen fingers digging into my flesh. I had a split second to think, *This is virtual reality. I shouldn't be able to feel him*, before he flung me across the room.

The curtain had been pulled back allowing me to fall full force onto his table of gore. The severed body parts of a young woman scattered on impact.

Both sliding in and sticking to fluids I didn't want to think about, I struggled to regain balance as another thought occurred to me. *If he can touch me, I can touch him.* Since the door I came through had disappeared, flight was no longer an option. Fight was all I had.

I whispered an apology to the dead young woman as I grabbed the blond hair of her detached head and swung it around over my own, releasing it with enough force to knock the cleaver from my attacker's hand. Without giving him time to recover, I grabbed one of her legs at the ankle (it only went to the knee), prepared to use it as a club. I lunged at the demon man, overshot my target, and slid in a puddle of blood just in time for him to grab my arm and pin it behind my back.

I craned my neck and saw a meat hook materialize in his once empty hand raised high above his head.

Hopelessness washed over me as I realized the game, this virtual reality world, was rigged. I couldn't win. There was only one way this could end.

I screamed as I felt the hook plunge into my stomach. I watched my own blood splatter against the wall as he tore the hook up and out of my midsection and hoped against all hope that I would faint.

He shoved me forward and I fell to my knees. I wanted to vomit, but it was a silly thought as I watched my guts and their contents fall to the floor from the gash in my torso.

Though strangely, I was aware of vomiting, just as I was aware of the visor being lifted and my body being freed of the virtual reality apparatus. I inspected my stomach. It was intact. Wiping vomit from my lips, I looked into the smug faces of the "good" doctors.

"How are you doing it," I asked through clenched teeth.

"Whatever do you mean?" One of them asked in mock innocence.

"How are you making us feel it, you sick sons of bitches?"

"Oh, honey," another smug bastard of a doctor began. "We're not sick. You are. But you're on the road to recovery now."

They helped me stand and I shrugged off their help as

soon as it sunk in that I actually hadn't been disemboweled and was physically intact. "Don't fucking touch me," I spat.

"It's a normal response to treatment," I heard the doctors confer as if I wasn't there. I was led, flanked but not touched, to a recovery room. A nurse directed me to a cushioned chair and hooked me to a machine to check my vitals. The machine beeped and another nurse recorded the readings, nodding as she went.

When they dispersed, I finally saw Mikey, ashen faced and clutching a bucket. The corner of his lip turned up in a weak smile, a pitiful shadow of the grin he'd worn during intake. He couldn't maintain it. "How?" he asked. It looked as if he wanted to say more but didn't have the strength.

"I don't know, but it's safe to say that we're not safe. We'll tell our parents," I said and then thought better of it, "or a child advocate or something."

"They won't believe us," came a voice from the corner. The voice was attached to a mousy-haired female who I hadn't noticed because she was crouched on the floor between the end of a row of chairs and the wall. She looked worse than Mikey and it was clear that even though she spoke, she had no intention of leaving her hiding place. "They never believe us. It's our word against doctors and experts. We're just mentally ill kids. Who would *you* believe?" Her voice lacked any trace of hope.

I knew she was right. My pulse quickened at the idea of telling my parents about what was happening here, or to request an advocate myself. The story was utterly unbelievable and therefore not likely to shorten my time at Sunrise. At the very least, I would just be doing more time at another facility treating delusions I didn't have. I was trapped. We were all trapped.

My only option was to survive the next three weeks in the facility the same way I had survived the previous seventeen years in my family home. I would gauge which emotional responses pleased my jailors and conduct myself accordingly; tell them what they wanted to hear. Lie.

That night, I evaded the demon man's hook by screaming myself awake. I stared into the darkness, shivering and covered in sweat, until a nurse who had heard me scream came to check on me. I worried, as she did a quick check of my vitals, that my nightmare betrayed my intentions. My nightmare turned out to be a good thing. Here, they wanted proof of emotion. They wanted it controlled, to be sure, but they wanted something they could measure. The kids who tried not to break would suffer the most torture.

It was new emotional territory, but I learned the

parameters in an impressive amount of time for someone who supposedly lacked empathy. I assumed the nurses and counselors agreed as they became increasingly careless around me.

One of the counselors, Laura, liked to use aroma therapy candles in our talk sessions. She usually put her lighter back in her pocket, but lately she would leave it on her desk. More than once the lighter sat within my reach as she walked around the room. Seeing as how they expected us to cut our meat with plastic knives, I guessed that access to lighters was forbidden too. Counselor Laura should have been more careful, but now was not the time to betray trust. Now was the time to play a part.

Once, a nurse put a pair of scissors down on the counter next to me and turned her back to fiddle with files on a touch screen. I winced at my own ideas about how I could have used her trust to my advantage.

Via a careless caseworker who thought nothing of leaving me alone in the room for "just a minute," I eventually got a glimpse of my files which confirmed my assumptions about my performance. According to my file, I was an exemplary patient, highly responsive to treatment. My ruse was working.

Various doctors treated patients at Sunrise, but each of

us had to meet with Dr. Albert Hill once. I thought back to the orientation video I watched in the car and guessed this had more to do with marketing than any real medical care. A doctor endorsed by Connor Wentworth himself signing off treatment was likely a big enough draw to the facility that Dr. Hill damn well needed to put his signature somewhere on each patient file.

I hated him immediately, from the way he scrunched his nose to adjust his glasses to his pudgy fingers swiping the touch screen as he told me to enter the office without ever looking at me. In fact, that's what I hated about him the most. He behaved as though it was beneath him to look at me. The entire session consisted of him asking questions about my progress and then speaking over my answers with barely a glance my way.

All I could concentrate on was getting the session over with until Dr. Hill said the words that triggered the change in me. "I see you're scheduled for your second VR treatment on Thursday morning—"

"What?" It was my turn to cut him off. "I thought I was making progress." I could hear the hope leaving my voice the way it had left the mousy-haired girl in the recovery room.

"You are, but…" I heard very little after that. The point,

though hidden in press packet verbiage about the caliber of care, was that my parents paid for the three week treatment cycle which included two virtual reality sessions. Clients got what they paid for. I was going to suffer and he was going to make money on it.

Except, I wasn't going to suffer. He was not putting me into another of their virtual reality horror worlds that I couldn't escape by simply waking up. I would have died for real first.

That night when I closed my eyes, I was back in that grimy room with the demon man. He was using his meat cleaver on the body on the table and when he looked at me he did it with Dr. Albert Hill's face. He stopped dismembering the body and held the cleaver out to me.

I took it.

As I rounded the table the body began to look familiar. I knew that curve of the hip, the wavy, chestnut hair sticky with blood. I took a final step, turned the lifeless head, and saw my own face staring back at me. "Do it," the purple lips of the dead me whispered.

I lifted the cleaver above my head and obliged the dead me, hacking away at her body as she and I both laughed.

I woke up laughing. Thankfully no one heard. If they had heard, I might have been watched a little more closely.

If it was decided that I needed to be watched more closely, Counselor Laura might have started being more careful about where she put her lighter and when she turned her back. The doors at Sunrise all read fingerprints for access, but once the fire alarm is tripped all locks are disabled. Without Counselor Laura, I could have never set the fire that opened the doors. I will never hurt Counselor Laura.

I put on a lab coat on my way out of the building to help blend in with the staff rather than the patients. In the dark and the smoke and the chaos it was easy to slip away. In the distance I heard them start the head count over. I cast a glance over my shoulder to make sure they hadn't counted one too many staff and put the pieces together.

No one was any the wiser but one person. One face behind shaggy hair and glasses regarded me with recognition. Mikey perked up as he saw me through the smoke and the distance and then smiled the brilliant grin from the waiting room as he directed attention away from me. I will never hurt Mikey.

I slipped through the dark to the back edge of the property where the tool shed was located. I heard sirens approaching and smiled at my luck. No one heard me as I smashed the lock with a rock.

Once inside, I assessed weapon options. It wasn't enough to escape. I needed to make them pay. My eyes scanned over rakes and chainsaws, shovels and axes but I needed something I could actually wield, something that felt good in my hand. I had quite a lot of work to do with whichever tool I chose.

Then I saw it. It wasn't a meat hook like the one from the virtual reality or any of my nightmares since, but it was a hook and I didn't much care what its original purpose had been. I knew how I was going to use it.

I smiled as I hid the hook under the lab coat and retreated into the shadow of the forest. I was right, nothing was ever that clean and crisp without hiding something sinister.

I made a wide circle in the dark that brought me just below the entrance gate. Every car that left Sunrise Treatment Facility would have to pass my hiding spot. I stayed hidden until I saw lights. As the lights came closer, I stepped out onto the side of the road and started to wander down the lane. I stroked the hook under my coat as I heard the car slowing down behind me.

"Mara?" I heard a voice that was too good to be true. I turned and saw Dr. Hill. His hands were still on the wheel and I took a moment to take note of the fact that he was driving manually. Control freaks always did. Again, my heart raced with anticipation. This was going to be sweet. "Mara, get in the car. The fire is under control and they're going to start letting you all back in now. I'll take you back."

"No," I said simply, knowing he would approach. He was not the kind of man who took no for an answer. I gripped the hook as I heard his car door open and shut.

"Mara," he said my name again. I felt his hand drop on my shoulder.

I grinned wide enough to put Mikey to shame as I turned on my heel and buried the hook in his abdomen. He wouldn't look at me before, but now his eyes were locked with mine and full of terror. "You made me what I am," I said and yanked the hook back out of his flesh, his organs spilling in actual reality the way mine had in virtual reality. "And every last one of you up to Connor Wentworth himself will get to meet your creation."

He tried to speak but only blood came from his mouth. I gave his head the same treatment I'd given his midsection and retreated back into the shadows to wait for the next.

Blood Money

I sat with my hands folded right over left on my lap. My black skirt was crooked and my mascara had run to my chin. It felt inappropriate to straighten my appearance. In my disarray, I fit right in with the morbid atmosphere of that room with the shades closed. The lack of light emphasized the dark maroon carpet and wooden panels stained mahogany. Why break the aesthetic? Even if I hadn't fit the picture quite so well, who would bring it to my attention during the reading of Aunt Belle's will?

My younger sister Katherine discreetly slid a small make-up compact and a tissue into my hand. I didn't accept her offering and forced her to take it back. She looked at me with disdain as if she couldn't understand why I refused, like this was the same as passing notes in class.

Katherine looked perfect, like one of Aunt Belle's porcelain dolls, polished and unable to shed tears. I assumed it was Katherine's job to be stoic, to appear unaffected. She married money right after college and had spent much of her time since then arming herself with physical perfection, flawless propriety, and juicy gossip so she could be an excellent pool side companion for the other rich wives. I wasn't sure it was the make-up in the compact that made her face look so fresh. Her eyes had barely misted over since Aunt Belle passed. I wanted to hate Katherine for that, especially in the moment, but I couldn't expect her to turn off her years of conditioning.

I gave my sister the benefit of the doubt and assumed that her tear free face was due to the fact that the reading of the will was a formality, and cool formality was Katherine's domain. Aunt Belle read us the will herself while she lay in that hospital bed, barely able to breathe. I struggled to come to terms with the fact that the frail woman before us was Aunt Belle. She had always been so strong and capable and aptly named, as she never appeared less than beautiful. Perhaps it was just this new frailty mingled with the yellow-orange glow of the sunset creeping between the blinds, but it felt like she was being called to the afterlife even then. Of course, Aunt Belle would not rest until we had all heard her wishes from her lips.

She and Uncle Allan had no children of their own; so after he died and Aunt Belle had no one to look after anymore, she took it upon herself to care for the rest of the family. We endured it because it seemed to give her a purpose. Aunt Belle never trusted anyone to do anything right. Naturally, she considered it her duty to read her own will.

I can hear her now. "If you want something done right, do it yourself," which would have been cliché if she hadn't added, "or hire someone who knows he's expendable." Then she would grin at Uncle Allan, who would only smile back and say, "I love you dear." Even after Uncle Allan died, she often smiled at the empty spot at the table, closing her eyes, and no one dared speak until she exhaled and opened them again. Katherine always thought that was "creepy," but these were the things I loved most about Aunt Belle. It was like she believed that her memories could make Uncle Allan be there with her again, and I wanted her to believe in that little bit of magic because then I could believe in it too.

The executor came to my portion of the will. I pretended to pay attention, but I already knew what was mine. Aunt Belle left me a few pieces of jewelry that Uncle Allan had given to her and her collection of stuffed animals, which was rather extensive.

It's those stuffed animals that I remember most. My eccentric aunt could never pass up anything cute that looked like it needed her, and so she collected them well into her old age. Uncle Allan traveled a lot, and sometimes when he was away, Mom and Dad would send Katherine and me to stay with Aunt Belle. My mother never admitted it, but I know that she was worried about her sister being lonely by herself in that big house.

I remember Aunt Belle tucking us in and kissing us goodnight. Sometimes after Katherine fell asleep, I would tiptoe out of my bed and go to Aunt Belle's room. She'd be sitting on the floor under the soft yellow glow of her lamp, fussing over those animals. Since I was a child, it didn't seem strange to me. It seemed pretty normal. She looked so lonely, and I talked to my stuffed animals when I felt alone. So I would step to her side and she would look up and smile at me. She never sent me back to bed. She would just put her arm around me and then we would go downstairs for tea. It made sense that I got those animals.

The executor directed his attention to Katherine and a hint of bitterness crept back into my soul. With the exception of the few things already marked for the rest of us, the entire estate went to her. It didn't seem fair. I was the one who called Aunt Belle every weekend just to talk about how nothing ever happened in my life. I was the one who endured all of the cute little nicknames she had for me—well into adulthood—and I smiled all the while because I thought it made me special. I was the one who became a writer because Aunt Belle was a writer and her books, her words, made me want to be just like her. I was the only one who hadn't thought she had gone completely insane after Uncle Allan passed away. And I don't think Katherine ever gave her a second thought. The only part of the estate I felt Katherine deserved was the collection of those polished porcelain dolls, as hard and as lifeless as her.

But then it wouldn't be the first time that an undeserving wretch in our family got everything in a will.

One weekend when I was a child, the family had gathered at Grandma and Grandpa's house because Great Grandmother was very ill. We knew she didn't have long. I was barely seven years old, and yet my memory is just like an old picture—sepia, but clear. The phone rang and we were told that she had passed. Grandma and Grandpa were in another room, but Aunt Belle, Uncle Allan, and Mom and Dad were all in the kitchen trying to get Katherine and me to finish our lunches. My mother mentioned something about Great Grandmother finally being dead, which I thought was horribly cruel at the time, but I kept listening, not saying a word, hoping for some reason for the cold side of my mother that I was witnessing. Sure enough, it was Aunt Belle who came through with an explanation.

"She's been sick for four years, Grandpa has been dead for five. She was so lonely in that hospital. I'm not sure that I can be sad," Aunt Belle said and put her coffee cup down close to me so I could sneak a sip. It was a common ritual between Aunt Belle and me, but this time I was listening too closely to the conversation to bother.

"Do you remember when we were kids and she would say, 'When I'm too old and sick to be of any use, promise me you'll shoot me'?" my mother asked.

"Of course I remember," Aunt Belle replied. "The times I went to the hospital to see her, the doctor kept asking me if I wanted to…I just couldn't bring myself to do it. She was my grandmother!" Aunt Belle started to cry and Uncle Allan held her. "But I guess Aunt Carol took care of that," Aunt Belle said with no attempt to conceal her bitterness.

My mother replied, "Well, what could we expect? Grandma left Aunt Carol everything. That woman has been itching to pull the plug ever since she found out what she was going to get!"

My small, seven-year-old voice cracked as tears trickled down my face. "I don't care how much stuff you guys give to me, I couldn't kill you."

My parents stared at me, shocked that I understood the situation, but Aunt Belle never underestimated my young mind. She simply released herself from Uncle Allan's arms to give me a hug and tell me that she knew I couldn't do such a thing. She told me that I was too sweet and innocent, but then she shot a glance at Katherine, two and a half years old in her high chair, refusing every bite of food my mother tried to give her. It was as if Aunt Belle knew what kind of person Katherine would grow up to be.

Then it dawned on me, as clearly as if Aunt Belle had whispered it in my ear. I could see her, happily reunited with Uncle Allan, releasing herself from his arms for just enough time to hold me and whisper one last secret. Yes, it was that clear to me, sitting there in that office, that smug look on Katherine's face, why Aunt Belle chose to read us her will, why she chose to let Katherine know she would inherit everything. After all, it was Katherine who gave the order to, "End Aunt Belle's pain." And for the first time since Aunt Belle read the will, I smiled at my sister. Aunt Belle did give me the most important pieces of her. She had only given Katherine blood money.

Masquerade

The gentle evening breeze rustled the gold and garnet leaves that clung to skeletal branches as he watched the sun dip lower behind them. In time, the chill would descend and the mild evening stir would make way for whipping wind that cut to the core. For the moment though, the air hummed with promise, life, energy, and the hopeful expectation that infected his town during a festival.

Of the elaborate festivals held throughout the year, all of the events put together couldn't meet the grandeur of the Fall Foolery Festival: a ten-day carnival complete with live shows, rides, wine and cider tasting, and some small-time gambling that generally got overlooked by the law. While no one wanted the festival to end, everyone looked forward to the final night—the Annual Halloween Masquerade Ball that packed the town square (or the recreation hall in the case of inclement weather), with an excited revelry that spilled into any of the white picket fence lined streets on which the music could still be heard.

He especially looked forward to the ball. He could put on a mask and no one would recognize him. They'd see his silver Venetian mask, dark hooded cloak, and soft leather gloves and take his mannerisms and appearance as an expression of innocent mystery and mischief in the spirit of the seasonal celebration. The scenes playing themselves out behind eyes partially hidden by the mask would remain his little secret. No one else would know what he had in mind for *her*, and so he could concentrate on his intentions.

He watched her from the shadow cast by the ticket booth. He *had to* touch her. He removed a glove and brushed past her closely enough to feel the satin and lace skirts of her gown caress his fingers. She hadn't noticed the difference between him and the hundreds in the crowd who might have brushed past her, but he knew that he had gotten too close too soon. He tightened with arousal at the fantasy of his hard, gloved hands pressing into her soft naked flesh, her sweat dampening her dark hair. He pushed the thought away and regained composure. *Why rush the game? Why risk raising her attention too soon?*

The feathers adorning her mask swayed in the breeze as she tilted her head and lifted a hand to her ear to better hear what a fellow reveler was saying. She tossed her head back in laughter. The movement caused the rhinestones on her champagne colored, corseted gown to catch the last light of sunset. Getting in the line for cotton candy just as the sun dipped below the horizon, she effortlessly made the transition from blazing in the sunset like a fire goddess to twinkling in the neon lights like a star. *Sparkle now, little diamond*, he thought, thankful that his grin was obscured by his mask. *You'll be in the rough later.*

He disliked kettle corn, but the booth provided a good vantage point. He got in the back of the line, and watched her as she ordered at the front of the cotton candy line a few booths away.

An elderly man leaned out the window of the cotton candy booth and presented a thin cardboard cone topped with a big pink puff. She slid a glove off of her slender hand, reached inside an ornate pouch and traded him a couple of bills for the offering of pure sugar.

Wicked temptress, he thought as she pulled a piece of fluff, brought it to her lips and let it melt on her tongue. She ate a few pieces and then sucked the sugar residue from the tips of her fingers before pulling more of it, getting sticky all over again. *She's playing dirty*, he reasoned as he indulged in new fantasies. She would experience heat and cold at his hands. She would learn which of his tools brought the greatest sting. She would feel how painful anticipation could be once she had become accustomed to a rhythm that he would stop and resume at his whim. She would scream before he gagged her and then he would blindfold her for good measure. *She's doing this to me on purpose. She has this coming.*

"Hey man," he was pulled from his reverie by the teenage boy working the kettle corn booth. He hadn't realized that he'd made it to the front of the line. "Large, medium, or small?" the teenager asked.

"Never mind," he said. He glanced behind and noticed that she had moved on. "I thought you had cider here too." He strode into the crowd before the kid could direct him to the other side of the same booth where they did, in fact, sell cider.

She had thrown him off his game. That had never happened to him before. When he caught her, he would redeem himself for his momentary lapse.

She couldn't have gotten far and her gown was hard to miss. Most of the women wore sparkles and glitter, but she had clearly gone through great effort to look like a fairy tale princess. He knew he could spot her from a great distance if he could just get a clear view past the crowd. *Ferris wheel. I'll find her from the top of the Ferris wheel.*

As he approached, he saw that he was right. He could

spot her from far away with the proper line of sight and the Ferris wheel would be a major player.

Fortune was with him. Looking up at the wheel from his place in line, he saw her and a friend stuck at the top while passengers at the bottom unloaded. The two rocked their car, giggling and exchanging cotton candy flavors. The ride operator yelled at them to stop rocking, and they did until the operator's attention was elsewhere, and then they began again like insolent school girls. *The operator isn't the only one watching you. He might let you slide, but I'll make you pay.*

Her car was three away from being emptied and reloaded when he saw her emphatic gesturing and read her lips exclaiming, "Oh my god!" He wondered what her friend had said when he heard the familiar guitar riff of a classic rock song that was still popular. Her friend hadn't said a thing. Now that the band had started he knew she would go to the dance floor. He thought about heading there first, but the night was still young and the floor would be empty until people visited the wine tasting booth a few more times for liquid courage. The last thing he wanted to be was obvious.

He retreated further into the shadows as the ride operator opened the gate to her car and let her and her friend out with a look of mild contempt. Jealousy tightened in his gut as he saw the dazzling smile she flashed the ride operator, lifting her mask to wink at him. Naturally, he melted in his cheap work boots and flashed a return smile.

She would pay for that too.

But not before she grabbed her friend's hand and made a mad dash in the direction of the stage, skirts a flutter. He sauntered behind them, but there was a nagging worry in the back of his mind. How would he get her away? He knew her well enough to know that there wasn't much that could tear her away from a dance floor. The stage area was bound to get crowded and was too much of a focal point anyway. The siren lure of alcohol might move her, but he saw her fill a flask and tuck it into a garter under her ample skirts. He hadn't seen her take a drink from it all night so he assumed she had plenty left. Maybe he could catch her on a dark trek to the restroom, but she would most likely bring her friend with her, possibly to share the contents of the flask.

Still, he resolved to find a way. He wouldn't lose the game, even if he had to go to extreme measures to win.

Five people graced the dance floor when he got there. Two women, one dressed as a peacock and the other dressed as some sort of feline, swayed and spun between pointing and laughing at the drunken antics of their two male escorts who had already lost most of their costume components.

And there she was, in that ornate champagne dress, dancing vibrantly, lifting her mask every so often to wipe away sweat. Her friend sat on one of the benches situated around the dance floor exchanging what he assumed was town gossip with the others who, for the moment at least, preferred sitting to dancing. His target was alone.

He felt impotent. She was so close, so oblivious to anything off of the dance floor, but in this scenario he was powerless. The feeling deepened as he saw a man approach her. The two leaned in to each other to exchange words and then lifted their masks ever so slightly. They hugged in obvious recognition.

He knew the man as a neighbor who he had noticed looking lustfully at his target more than once. He often envisioned tearing this man's throat out for it too. It didn't help that he didn't like this neighbor. *Just give me an excuse to kick your ass,* he thought. *And seriously, would it kill you to mow your damn lawn?*

He recognized the intro to a Southern rock song that his target clearly liked in spite of the poor rendition by the festival band. She shook her hips and shoulders, seemingly uninhibited by the corset she wore. The neighbor watched her for a couple of seconds before moving on to a small group of women at the edge of the stage, presumably to convince them to dance. *You just saved your own life, buddy*, he thought.

He watched his target for a time he couldn't measure, fighting waves of his arousal the more he entertained his fantasies. As she spun and whirled and twirled around the dance floor under stars which could barely be seen past the festival lights, he imagined her bound in the dark, eyes wide and searching. *Oh, what I will do with you then!* For the moment, he could do no more than watch and wait.

Finally, breathing heavily and removing her mask to fully wipe the sweat from her face, she left the dance floor and rejoined her friend on the bench. She tied the ribbons of her mask together and slid it over her wrist with her pouch before taking the water bottle her friend offered her. She put the bottle to her lips and tilted her head back to take a long drink before returning the bottle and her attention to her friend.

She rubbed her arms vigorously. One of the men who had joined the women offered her the cape from his costume. She shook her head and checked her watch. Was she planning to leave?

She stood and hugged her friend. *Yes, she's planning to leave*, he reasoned. It was just as well as the crowd at the dance floor grew ever thicker and she had hardly been alone all night. He pulled the hood of his cloak down and fiddled with his gloves until she was well past him, and then got up and slipped into the night after her.

People walked, stumbled, ran, and even danced up and down the well-lit streets she had chosen to take. Already at the next corner and well ahead of him, she stopped and looked down the alley, presumably contemplating taking the shortcut he knew was there. She rubbed her arms against the chill and looked over her shoulder.

Pretending to inspect the bright red leaves of a sapling behind a hedge, he relied on his peripheral vision to see which way she would go. After another moment of inspecting the streets, she decided to continue on straight, keeping to the brighter path. *Smart woman*, he thought. *I knew I chose you for a reason.* He took the shortcut.

He slipped into the house through the back and crept through the kitchen into the front room where he could see her coming up the walk through the window or hear her coming through the back. He crouched beside the couch, eyes just above the window sill so he could watch the sidewalk.

Only a moment or two passed before she came into his line of site. She stopped under the street light, fished her keys from her pouch, and held the set up in the light to select the proper key before turning onto the front walk. *This is it.* She stopped halfway up the walk and looked around her again. *I'm not there, sweet thing. I'm here. And you will know it soon enough. You will* feel *it soon enough.*

He crouched lower and more tightly to both the wall and the couch, making himself as small and hidden as he could while waiting to hear the key slide into the lock.

She walked through the door and closed it behind her before flipping the dim foyer light.

"Baby? You home?" she called. "Babe!"

He heard her snicker before crossing the room to enter the kitchen, oblivious to his presence. "Looks like I won," she said. He came up behind her as she dropped her keys on the kitchen counter.

"Gotcha" he hissed, grabbing her. She yelped as he spun her around and bent her backwards against the counter. Her chest heaved as he clapped his hand over her mouth. "I win," he whispered in her ear and toyed with the laces of her corset.

***

"I still maintain that you didn't win this year since you didn't catch me until I got into the house," she said from her vulnerable position as he untied the smooth ropes binding her wrists to the bedposts.

"What if I told you I didn't use my key to get in?" he asked, the playful lilt in his tone that he often found himself using with his wife.

"Then we have to upgrade our security tomorrow," she said firmly, rubbing her newly freed wrists. "The idea of someone stalking me on Halloween for real is just...ugh!" She shivered and wrapped a sheet around her naked body.

"There's no need to worry," he said and bent to kiss her forehead and stroke her hair. "I cheated and used my key and you won the game this year."

"And yet you still got a prize," she said with playful sarcasm. "Imagine that."

"Yeah," he snorted, matching her sarcasm as he pulled his boxer shorts on. "Because your prior screaming indicated that you would have preferred a toaster to what we just did."

He watched the red rise in her face. He delighted in the fact that he could still make her blush after ten years of marriage.

Waiting Room

Too bright, Amy thought as she sat in the waiting room. *Too stark, like overexposed film.* She shifted in her seat and smoothed her clothing, unable to shake the feeling that she'd been there before, though she didn't know how she'd gotten there to begin with. She rubbed the scars healing on her wrist and wondered if her lapse in memory and accompanying sense of déjà vu were part of her recent emotional break.

She racked her brain, trying to retrace her steps. She remembered sitting in her bi-weekly, out-patient group therapy session, a sad face among sad faces, feeling them judge her as she spoke. *Poor woman!* She could hear them thinking, the voices she imagined thick with cruel sarcasm. *How horrible it must be to have a successful career and a nice apartment uptown! What right does she have to misery?* It didn't matter how many times they had all been told that careers and apartments didn't necessarily bring happiness. At the end of the day, she felt judged for being perceived as having it easier than most.

She tried to tell them about the loneliness, how nothing she had was worth a damn without people she loved and trusted to share it with. Even still, their expressions seemed to boil her suffering down to, *Poor ex-prom queen, doesn't have a boyfriend? Yes. Yes. Certainly slash your arms open for that, you idiot!*

There was only one face that appeared soft and compassionate to her, one face onto which she couldn't project her own fears of judgment. Perhaps that's why, when he came up to her after the session, she hadn't laughed at the business card he offered.

It was a laughable concept. "Forever Fix-It. We undo what's been done," the card read. Then in small print, "One time and one change only." She wondered just how serious some of the disorders in the group were before accepting the card.

Taking the card was the last thing she remembered before her arrival in the waiting room. The only door led to wherever people were being called after their wait. She could not locate an exit. It occurred to her that she should be afraid, but perhaps the sense of familiarity suppressed the emotion. She was uncomfortable in the chair, under whelmed with the reading material, and annoyed to be waiting, but not afraid.

"So what're you gonna change?" came a gruff voice from beside her. She swore there hadn't been anyone there a second ago.

"I haven't thought about it," she lied. She would not lament the circumstances of her life to a man with only one leg. She wasn't in session now; she didn't have to share. "What about you?"

"No more cutting firewood drunk," he said, his chuckle reaching his bright eyes.

"A worthy change," she agreed.

"I think that was part of the criteria to get here," he said with a knowing smile. "So tell me then, what are you going to change?"

Her right to misery validated, she thought back to the many nights spent lying awake, thinking about her life and how it turned out the way it had. She pinpointed one event: accepting the job at the magazine.

Of course, it wasn't that simple. She loved her job. There was no question about that, nor could anyone question her dedication as she often worked into the wee hours, either at the office or at home. It was what she had to do to excel and the awards cluttering the mantel proved her efforts a success. However, professional fulfillment wasn't the same as love, and she'd begun to regret those late nights at the office that could have just as easily been spent laughing with friends, or holding a boyfriend, or maybe even tucking her children safely into bed. It was the loneliness that was killing her.

It was her own fault. After consistently telling her friends she had work to do, they invited her out less and less frequently until they stopped altogether. Her romantic life never got off the ground. She would go to dinner or have cocktails with a guy and then never find enough space in her schedule to cultivate a relationship. Since she hadn't had time for friends or romance, the idea that she'd have time for children was ludicrous.

"Amy Watson?" The voice of an agent pulled her from her thoughts.

"Here," she said.

"We're still looking for your file. It should just be another minute."

She started daydreaming about what her new life was going to be like. Would she be going out with a group of friends that night? Maybe she'd snuggle under a blanket watching a movie with her family, not caring that the children keep spilling butter on the sofa. No matter what the daydream, she saw herself with people she would love dearly.

"Ms. Watson."

"Yes," she answered excitedly. Her excitement dimmed a bit when she saw the agent's expression.

"I found your file. I'm afraid I have some news."

"News?"

"Yes. There's been a mix-up with your paperwork. You see, I'm afraid we can't help you. We know you don't remember; in fact, that's our policy, but this isn't the first time you've been here."

"I don't understand."

"We had trouble finding your file because you were Mrs. Amy Jensen then, not Ms. Amy Watson. It wasn't until we typed 'Watson' into the proper maiden name field that we found your file and caught our error. We're sorry for having contacted you again."

"But that's just not possible. You made a mistake before, this could be another."

"This isn't a mistake. Um, let's see." He flipped through the file. "Yes, you felt unfulfilled in your life and wanted to go back and…"

"Take the job at the magazine," she finished for him. "I know."

An exit door appeared to her right and her heart sank with the finality of it. The realization that a new life could be so simple to acquire in this mysterious place, but that she'd already used her chance and still could not find happiness threatened to crush her under a depression the likes of which she had never felt.

Her only solace as she headed for the exit door was that she was already beginning to forget.

Nightmares

Fear. Nathan McNeal realized he'd never truly felt it. The idea of being frozen with fear, or rendered temporarily incontinent with terror, had been so foreign to him that he thought them to be no more than hyperbolic expressions. Yet he experienced them both in the eternal second it took him to realize that the blaring horn was meant to alert him, and that the oncoming headlights were in his lane.

Darkness. It bothered him as a child and it still made him uneasy, but he was an adult now. He comforted himself with the thought that darkness was better than the bright light reported by those who had tasted death but had been sent back to their lives for some reason. He wouldn't be sent back, given a second chance to fix the things he saw as his life flashed before his eyes, which, come to think of it, also hadn't happened. He wasn't dead.

He wasn't dead. That realization should have come with a sigh of relief, but the fear crept back in. Why couldn't he move? What was the source of the steady beeping that was driving him mad? And why was he certain that something horrible waited for him in the inky darkness?

Focused on breathing evenly, he tried to assess his situation. *It's just the dark. The dark can't hurt you*, Nathan thought to himself, though he felt the fear begin to swell in his stomach. *Don't let your imagination get the better of you. Must be realistic about these things.* The thought was his, but it came in his mother's voice. His mother was right. He swallowed, willing himself to quell the fear that grew with each infernal beep. He couldn't move and when he tried to open his mouth, he found that he couldn't scream. Fear clawed at his insides as the beeping seemed to get faster.

At precisely the moment he knew he couldn't take any more, a bottom he hadn't been aware of dropped out and he started to fall. *Just hold on, Nathan.* The whisper came from somewhere in the distance and there was nothing to hold on to. There was just him, falling in the blackness.

He wasn't sure how long he fell, but eventually he felt a crushing jolt to his body as it stopped abruptly, hitting cold, hard ground. As he fought to catch his breath, he could feel grass tickling his arms, a stone wedged underneath his shoulder, and dew clinging to his skin. He could hear an acoustic guitar being poorly played, accompanied by young voices. Surprised at his ability to move, he ran his hands over dried leaves, crushing them between his fingers. Lured by the smell of wood smoke and the sound of laughter, he opened his eyes and sat up with ease.

He knew this place. This was Camp Tomahawk. He had been a boy scout as a youngster, and the two weeks spent at Camp Tomahawk at the end of the summer made all the work on merit badges and soap box derby cars well worth it. Around the campfire sat his boyhood friends: Tommy, Joe, and Fat Luke, who was actually rail thin, but ate like a full grown man with a tape worm. Even though they had their backs to him, he would have known Rusty, Shy Tim, and Johnny Mischief anywhere. Scoutmaster Mark sat on a high stump telling a ghost story, and strummed his guitar when he thought music could intensify the mood.

Nathan took his place on a stump across from Scoutmaster Mark, and impaled a marshmallow at the end of a thin stick that had been whittled to a point, making a fine skewer. If there was a heaven, this was it.

Scoutmaster Mark dropped his voice to a whisper and looked over his shoulders. A master not only of scouts, but also of story-telling, he knew just how to make the boys shiver at the tale of One-Eyed Jack. A victim of a horrible prank gone wrong in these very woods, One-Eyed Jack stalked campsites, taking the eyes of boys who misbehaved to place in his own empty, rotted eye socket. Shadows danced on Scoutmaster Mark's face in the firelight, and as he described One-Eyed Jack's first kill, it seemed he was speaking directly to Nathan. Scoutmaster Mark's face darkened and twisted in a sick grin.

Nathan looked around the campfire to the other boys. Tommy, Joe, and Rusty sat forward on their stumps, enthralled with the tale. Shy Tim rocked back and forth with his arms wrapped around his knees. The poor boy would have nightmares this evening. Fat Luke gulped the end of a hotdog, placed another on the end of his skewer, and shoved it into the fire. Johnny Mischief placed a spider in the hood of Fat Luke's sweatshirt while he was paying more attention to the hotdog than to him. If any of them had noticed a change in their Scoutmaster, they weren't showing it.

Scoutmaster Mark nodded at a space behind Nathan's shoulder. Refusing to be afraid, Nathan turned around. One-Eyed Jack stood there grinning at him, one eye fixed on his. His empty eye socket oozed puss, and fat maggots ate the rotted flesh. He raised a gleaming knife and rushed at Nathan.

Nathan took a defensive stance, intending to throw One-Eyed Jack over his shoulder and into the fire. One-Eyed

Jack, too clever to be bested by that maneuver, took a flying leap, coming down on Nathan hard, pinning him to the ground. Nathan called for help, looking around at his friends with pleading eyes. Johnny Mischief pointed and laughed at Fat Luke slapping at his neck to try and kill the spider. Shy Tim continued rocking back and forth, terrified of the story. Tommy, Joe, and Rusty stared at Scoutmaster Mark, who was the only one who seemed to notice the struggle going on between Nathan and One-Eyed Jack. Scoutmaster Mark watched intently as if he'd placed a bet on the battle, grinning as though his was the smart money.

One-Eyed Jack's knife point edged closer to Nathan's left eye. Nathan gripped One-Eyed Jack's knife hand, pushing as hard as he could to get the knife away, but he was outmatched.

One-Eyed Jack raised his knife in victory over him, Nathan's left eye and much of what connected it to his brain dangled from the knife point and glistened in the firelight. With his remaining eye, Nathan watched in horror as One-Eyed Jack bit into the eye he'd stolen, fluid squirting in all directions. "Don't fret, boy," One-Eyed Jack said. "This be your left eye. I'm missin' m'right!" One-Eyed Jack lifted his gleaming blade again.

Nathan threw his arms over his face and braced himself.

"And you thought *I'd* be scared!" a sweet voice teased. Nathan dropped his arms and opened his eyes—both of them—to his high school sweetheart, Alyssa. The lights from the drive-in movie screen flickered on her youthful face.

Like Camp Tomahawk, he recognized this. He had brought Alyssa to the late showing of the re-mastered version of *The Exorcist* in the hope that fear might put her in the snuggling mood. Nathan doubted that the image of a tortured Linda Blair vomiting pea soup could put anyone in that kind of mood, but Johnny Mischief swore it worked like a charm with his own girlfriend the week earlier.

Alyssa snuggled in close to him and rested her head on his chest. He stroked her silky, blond hair. It smelled of strawberries with a faint hint of cigarette smoke. They were teenagers, after all, and smoking a couple of cigarettes wasn't the worst thing people their age did at the drive-in. The night's crisp air faded and turned stale, as a stronger, more acrid scent took the place of strawberries and cigarettes. It reminded him of the time a mouse got caught behind his bedroom wall and never got free again. He shifted in his seat to crack the window. He didn't want Alyssa to notice the smell which would surely ruin the mood.

She ran her slender hand across his chest to his

shoulder. "Don't worry, Nathan," she whispered. "Nothing is going to possess you while I'm around." Her hand suddenly seemed to burn. He looked at her and watched her face contort, jaws unhinging, showing rows of dagger-like fangs. "Nothing will possess you," said the demon voice that came from the cracking waste that had once been Alyssa's lips. "Because you're already mine!"

Then she was upon him, clawing at his skin, ripping through muscle and viscera with her teeth. As he struggled against the agony of being torn apart, he saw his own blood splatter on the windshield while more substantial parts of him congealed in globs on the dashboard. Through the blood in his eyes, he saw her lift his heart in her clawed hand and edge it in cinematic slow motion to her unhinged jaw before he fell into blackness once more.

"Nathan," he heard someone call in the distance. "Nathan…Mr. McNeal!"

He jerked awake to the glare of bright fluorescent lights. "Huh?" His eyes focused on the impatient face of Ms. Anderson, the instructor of his 400 level Comparative Literature college course.

"Hopefully you can stay awake through your own presentation, Mr. McNeal. And hopefully you will move us enough to treat you with more consideration than you've shown your classmates today."

He gathered his notes and stood up. Making no attempt to explain how he'd pulled an all-nighter to wow them with his presentation, he made his way to the front of the class. It wasn't his classmates he wanted to wow. Ms. Anderson had starred in more than one of his erotic daydreams with her red, polished nails and dark hair styled in a way that reminded him of the femme-fatal in old film noir flicks. Admittedly, falling asleep in her class wasn't the best way to impress her, but his presentation would do the trick.

His legs felt rubbery as he stole a glance at her shapely calves. He forced himself to focus, recognizing this as his own nervous aversion to public speaking. It was part of why he'd been up all night, polishing his work, willing his careful preparation to supersede his nerves.

He remembered the old bit of advice to picture everyone in their underwear. He would do that for everyone except Ms. Anderson. Picturing Ms. Anderson in her underwear would have him babbling like a fool.

Focus, Nathan, he thought, in a voice too far away to be his own. After convincing himself that the audience was clad only in undergarments, he directed his attention to his first note card, so blurred and smudged he could barely read it. The more he squinted and tried to focus, the less he could make out. His mouth went dry as he realized he couldn't remember anything that had been written on them.

He looked out over the classroom full of students. They were clothed again and laughing. Some pointed at him; others covered their eyes, but they all laughed. He looked down and realized he was the one who was naked.

He tried to cover himself, his bony chest, concave stomach, skinny legs. He hadn't blossomed physically until months later after he'd purchased a gym membership and embraced free weights and protein drinks. He tried to cover it all, but he only had two hands.

Ms. Anderson pointed and laughed along with all of them.

You're supposed to be supportive, empowering. You're supposed to know how much I need you.

Then, to his horror, the hands that covered him grew black, festering sores. He couldn't hide the sores and himself at the same time. He watched as those sores grew bigger and spread to other parts of his body.

The manhood his hands had been hiding from view caught the infection first. He watched, wide-eyed and open-mouthed as it rotted and fell to the floor. The class roared with laughter. The few muscles he had rotted next, as he collapsed under pain and lack of strength.

The Comparative Literature class continued to laugh as Ms. Anderson lectured on the falls of Hercules and Achilles. She commented on how Mr. Nathan McNeal had hardly been either, but his decomposition was the best example they had. She assigned a paper comparing what they were seeing in front of them to what they had read—no more than five pages, no less than three. He was rotting and dying and not a soul cared. He crouched in the fetal position, eyes pinched shut, and put what remained of his hands over his ears, chanting all the while, "Stop, stop, stop!"

"Stop, stop, stop!" he was still chanting when he felt someone shaking his shoulder.

"Nate," the whisper came. "Nate!"

It was still a whisper, but one full of dread.

"Nate," his wife whispered. "Nate."

"What, honey?" he said, groggily letting go of his nightmare. "What is it?"

"I heard something downstairs," Elizabeth said. She leaned over him, her dark hair disheveled, a crusted drool trail running from her full lips to her adorable round chin. She was beautiful. "Someone's breaking into the house."

He remembered this too. Elizabeth had a fondness for eerie entertainment. She'd been raised on *The Twilight Zone*, *Unsolved Mysteries*, and B level horror films. She swore she loved it, but every time she watched a marathon of shows or movies of a darker nature, she'd also end up swearing someone was breaking in and trying to kill them in the middle of the night.

He refused to pander to her fears. "You know where the baseball bat is," he said. She grabbed it from under the bed. He expected her to return, swinging at shadows as she always did.

This time she returned with the grubby hands of a masked man around her neck. He choked her with every step.

Panic filled her wide eyes as she stumbled into the room, her every move controlled by an unknown madman. He had a gun, and he pointed it at Nathan's face.

"Do as I say, and you'll survive," the man said.

Nathan froze, seeing nothing but the frightened eyes of his wife. He wanted to fight, but perhaps the best way to save her was to give in. She was his everything. He had to be smart.

"Everything worth something is in the safe. I'll give you the combination. Just don't hurt her," he said.

"We didn't want to hurt her," he said as a smaller man came through the bedroom door, a screwdriver in his hand. "We wanted to hurt you, and now you've let us know that hurting her is how to hurt you."

She let out a scream as the second man thrust his screw driver into a non-lethal part of her abdomen.

Sweat poured down her face as Nathan lunged at the men, putting his all into saving his Elizabeth.

The meaty fist of the first man knocked him into the wall.

The second man threw the bleeding Elizabeth to the floor and cut her clothes from her flesh. She lay naked and shivering inches from Nathan and he could barely move. He reached out his hand, and the first man grabbed his wrist. The man produced a saw out of nowhere and began cutting Nathan's arm off at the elbow. Every stroke with the saw produced fresh stars in his vision, but he fought to stay conscious. If he passed out, they would kill Elizabeth.

There was one last stroke of the saw before the first man raised Nathan's arm above his head and let out a whoop of celebration. Nathan turned away, gripping his bloody stump as the men began to beat Elizabeth with the detached arm. She fought and scratched, but the more she fought and scratched, the more furiously they beat her.

"Watch!" they screamed at Nathan, but he refused. Maybe if he refused to watch, they'd let her be.

Then the closet doors opened, and out came One-Eyed

Jack.

"He'll watch," he said to the men. Then he turned to Nathan. "Don't worry, boy," he said. "I'm not here t' blind ya. I'm here to make y' see." Then One-Eyed Jack took his gleaming blade and pried the eyes out of Nathan's skull, resting them on his cheeks to make him watch the murder of the love of his life no matter how hard he pinched his lids shut.

***

It went on that way, over and over again. "Make it stop!" Nathan cried, lying in the fetal position in the darkness. "What have I done to deserve this?" He didn't know how long he'd been in this hell, watching every good part of his life turned to torment flash before his eyes. "Please, God! Make it stop!"

***

"You've got to stop this," Nathan's mother said to Elizabeth in the stark, sterile hospital room where she'd been living for months. "He wouldn't want this. He wouldn't want life in a coma or some vegetative state. He wouldn't want you to spend everything you've saved and run yourself into financial ruin trying to keep him alive. He's not going to wake up!" She took Elizabeth by the shoulders and continued. "I'm his mother and I'm saying this. I love my son more than life itself, but this isn't life, and you have to let go. Please cut the life support and stop prolonging this."

"But I swear I saw his eyes flutter," Elizabeth responded. "I swear I saw life. I know you told me not to let my imagination get the better of me and to be realistic about these things, but I have faith he'll hold on. He'll come out of this. He won't let go. He'll come back to me."

And in his mind, Nathan began another nightmare.

Silver in the Moonlight

David sat in the corner of the coffee shop waiting for Diana's arrival. Like many of the patrons, he sat with his laptop open, pretending to be focused on the screen. He didn't need to go over the articles again as he'd already been through the stories of wild animal sightings and organized hunts with a fine toothed comb. Stories of sightings always hit the local paper around the full moon, while the advertised dates of the organized hunts always fell during some other moon phase.

He wasn't sure whether that was fortunate or unfortunate. On one hand, he could certainly be grateful that the townspeople weren't traipsing through the woods hunting for something that they could never understand and for which they were totally unprepared. On the other, this most likely meant that there was a werewolf on the board of the sportsmen's club that organized the hunt.

He had known there was a werewolf in the little New England town for a while and had been willing to stay away, giving it the benefit of the doubt. He wasn't a monster himself, after all. He wasn't one of the hunters who would shoot and kill without question and sell werewolf pelts to high paying occult collectors. No. That wasn't him. He knew that, with the exception of the night of the full moon, a werewolf was a person, just like him.

He resolved to watch and wait, but it wasn't long before it became clear that he had to pay a visit to the fishing village nestled between the North Atlantic and thick forest.

It started like any other night. The sound of a sportscaster analyzing an important play competed with the sound of the traffic coming through the open windows of his tiny bachelor pad. He had just placed a bowl of soup in the microwave and returned to stirring his instant stuffing, craning his neck to look from the stove to the television and back again, when he heard the ping of his Google alerts. He removed the pot from the heat, turned off the burner, and brought his screen back to life. Memories of Julia, his dead sister, flooded his mind as he read about the 22-year-old girl who had been attacked. His sister had been 22. Unlike Julia, this girl would live, but he knew what she would become. How could he trust her to control herself and take necessary safety precautions when the wolf who nearly killed her hadn't maintained enough control not to attack a human in the first place? Now there would be two werewolves, maybe more.

Finding it wasteful to throw food away, he choked down his stuffing and chicken soup from a can while running a mental checklist of everything he'd need for his journey and stay in Massachusetts and for his hunt there. He was grateful, as he studied the picture accompanying the article that this girl, Diana, with her mocha latte complexion and long, dark springing curls, looked nothing like his sister. It would make it much easier for him to fire the shot, punching one of his custom silver bullets through her heart.

He started slightly as the imagined sound of gun blast jolted him back to the world of the coffee shop. He reviewed his mental checklist again as he feigned writer's block, staring at his blank computer screen and sipping his coffee.

The bell above the door jingled as his target walked through wearing a short sundress and a chipper smile.

"Hey, Diana!" the girl behind the counter called. "Want your usual?"

David recognized her name from the article about her attack. The scar on her thigh, kissed gently by the hem of her sundress, confirmed her identity.

"Hey, Sadie! Yeah, I'll take my usual and Annie's too," Diana answered.

"Oh, you're just on a break? I thought you were getting out early today."

"I am, but I feel bad about it. We just got a big shipment of books, and our hoogie-woogie trinket shipment came in with half of the stuff broken. I'm bringing her coffee to alleviate my guilt."

Yes, she would be leaving work early on the night of the full moon. David put another check in the identity confirmed column of his mental checklist and watched as she plunked her purse on the counter and fished for her wallet while the girl behind the counter set to steaming milk.

She turned and caught him staring at her thigh. He began to mouth the word "sorry" when her expression changed. Or he thought it did. He could have sworn he saw recognition. Had she noticed him following her? No. She couldn't have. A woman who had recognized a stalker would be either angry or frightened, and she looked neither. He broke eye contact and directed his gaze back to his screen. He heard the girl behind the counter say, "Here ya go."

He peeked through his dirty blonde hair, which hung in his face to conceal his eyes. Diana, both hands full, pushed the door open with her hip. He knew she'd cross the street to New England New Age, the book store where she worked.

He also knew she was only dropping off coffee. It gave him no more than a minute to pack up his belongings and be outside doing what would appear to be no more than stepping out for a smoke when she left again.

***

Diana took a familiar path into the woods as the last rays of the day's sun grew dimmer. Her finger itched and tingled under the silver ring she wore. She pulled it off, admiring the moon and stars pattern etched into it before she slid it into the pocket of her denim shorts. She sighed as she lifted her hand to the last light of the day to inspect the band of red irritation around her ring finger. She considered that maybe it was time for a new good luck charm, and then promptly reconsidered. She had, after all, survived a brutal attack on the very night the ring was given to her.

The first wave of power rolled up her spine letting her know that the transformation would soon come. She shivered as the sensation rolled back down and an almost giddy grin came to her face. She no more controlled her changes than she controlled anything else in nature, but it always made her feel powerful and free.

Diana took the elastic from her hair and shook it out.

She always did that first. Then she unfastened her shorts and let them slide down her athletic legs to the forest floor and then pulled her tank top off over her head. Once she slipped free of her undergarments, she tucked them into her shorts and rolled her clothes into a ball which she placed in a hole in a nearby tree trunk. Stepping naked and barefoot into the clearing, she felt the soft ferns brush her calves with every step across velvety green moss. Moths and various other nighttime insects fluttered up and landed on other, undisturbed vegetation. Crickets and peepers called to each other as birds came home to roost, chattering noisily in the trees.

She'd never felt more connected to nature than she had in the past couple of months. In that moment, smelling the intoxicating, sweet and spicy scent of the forest, she couldn't understand why her condition had been referred to—through years of books of fiction and horror movies—as a curse. If those writers had known how she felt, they'd have written their stories differently.

She remembered that she hadn't felt that way at first, as her fingers traced the ragged scar on her thigh. It happened on the night she first decided to join a new group of friends in the woods for a spiritual meeting which would include a bonfire and naked moonlight dancing. She'd felt some trepidation about doing such a thing, but Annie, her friend and the manager of the local New Age shop, was anxious for her to be initiated into the coven. She'd even let her have a sneak peek at the silver moon and stars ring that each one of them received when they became full members. Diana told herself that the anxiety that settled into her gut and stayed there all through that day was ridiculous. She'd never felt more welcomed and loved by any group of people, especially those who held to any type of religion, than she had with the coven, these people who embraced a strict *Harm None* policy and a strong respect for nature and the connection of all living things.

Diana had never felt more alive than she had before she almost died. She'd almost reached the end of the path back out of the woods, exhilarated by the night's experiences and feeling a very true and deep love for her new brothers and sisters, when the wolf came out of nowhere. At first, she didn't even register it was a wolf. It was simply a huge and hairy beast that hit like lightening slamming into her and knocking her to the ground. She fought against the stars springing up in her vision and almost wished she hadn't when she focused on the snarling wolf muzzle. Drool dripped from its fangs onto her face and into her eyes. She didn't dare wipe it away. At that point, simply fighting—the act of survival—was more important than seeing. She struggled to catch her breath, to scream for help, but upon feeling the tearing in her thigh, her fight was rendered futile. The last thing she remembered was of the sound of her friends screaming before she blacked out.

She'd been stitched up that night and released from the hospital the next day, but the nightmares, cold sweats, shakes, and strange cravings for raw meat followed the bite and got worse. She'd heard some of the older members of her moonlight group whispering about home remedies, and had been forced to drink a number of foul teas, but nothing helped. She didn't understand what was happening to her until *he* tracked her down.

"My name is Adam. I'm the wolf that bit you," he said and dropped his head. "I'm so sorry, but I'm here to help you through it and eventually you'll get used to it. You may even really like it. A lot of us do."

So this was what she got for trying something new. Had her anxiety been a warning?

She shook her head. She didn't want to believe him, but her new and improved sense of smell told her he spoke truth. The power she sensed behind his green eyes—eyes that had a ring of amber close to their pupils—confirmed what she smelled on him. An otherworldly strength emanated from his broad shoulders, making it easy for her to picture his mop of sandy brown hair as thick wolf fur.

Although she'd adopted a *Harm None* philosophy, she very much wanted to kill him; however, the desire to do violence lasted only until the night of her first change. The morning after her first transformation, she crawled to where Adam lay on the forest floor and kissed his cheek. He'd given her a gift, albeit by accident, and she embraced her newest set of moonlight friends. Her pack.

The second wave of power rolled up and down her spine, bringing her back to the present. It wouldn't be long now. She'd endure mind-numbing pain, but come out on the other side more powerful, connected to an ancient line at one with nature and the full moon above.

She stood on her tiptoes and raised her arms to the sky, taking one last stretch in her human body before the change took her.

The third wave was upon her. The change always swept her legs out first, knocking her to her knees before the bones of her legs reformed themselves. She watched her hands scratching at the dirt in anguish as they twisted into claws. In that moment, she pondered which was more her, the hand or the claw. The human never fully left the wolf, and likewise the wolf never fully left the human. The wolf could, if she wanted, form a human thought; the human could, if she wanted, be absolutely primal, even beastly.

Both the human and the wolf allowed a tortured growl to escape as shoulder blades tore flesh and the spine extended past the tail bone to an actual tail. Somewhere in their collective mind they knew that the pain, that was somehow also a form of relief, was coming to an end. If they could just last a few more seconds, they would be running with the wind, seeing the earthy, green blur of ferns and brambles as they raced by. In seconds, just as expected, the torment ended.

They lifted their muzzle to the sky and howled in triumph, the howl the final seal completing the transformation.

The she-wolf had barely caught the scent when she heard the shot. It went wide, embedding a silver bullet in a tree. Before the human part could force a thought, the wolf took off at a full sprint through the underbrush.

***

David sensed his dead sister smiling upon him as he climbed the tree stand in the fading twilight. Tree stands served as useful vantage points for deer hunters during buck or doe season. He wondered if this was the first time it had been climbed as part of a werewolf hunt.

If it was fortuitous that he'd found a tree stand, it was even more so that when he directed his attention to a slight rustling sound, he saw Diana, just under a hundred yards away, step into a patch of ferns.

He felt more than a little like a peeping tom watching her shake out her long dark hair and undress before the change. He reasoned that he couldn't be certain she was a werewolf unless he saw the moment she shifted.

If he'd had even a whisper of doubt in his mind before, it was gone when the first jolt of her transformation knocked her to the ground. He watched as bones shifted and rolled under human flesh that was quickly covered in dark fur the color of the cascading tresses that fell between human shoulder blades only seconds before.

He lifted his rifle and watched the rest of her transformation through his night vision scope. He would not fire a shot until she was fully transformed, and he would know the transformation was complete when he heard the howl.

He whispered an apology and pulled the trigger. He missed, and the wolf was on the run.

"Damn," he muttered as he began his descent from the

tree stand. He reminded himself that it wasn't the first time he'd missed a shot. He missed the first shot on his very first hunt too, when he went after his sister's killer. That night still ended with a dead wolf. This time would be no different. His feet hit solid ground. "Let the chase begin," he said to the forest around him as he set off in the direction his target had run.

***

Run a circle. Double back. Larger circle in the other direction.

The wolf had no problem navigating the forest, but Diana, the passenger inside the wolf, took a mental note of every direction run. Tonight's task was too important for her to take her usual back seat, enjoying the wild freedom of her wolf form. Primal instinct alone would not get the job done. She needed her diabolical human brain and her wolf's instinct to work in tandem. Her ability to marry the two was stronger in her than it was in the other members of her pack and was considered her special talent, the reason she was chosen for the task in the first place. It was why she wore clothes that revealed her scars, and thus her identity, giving the hunter every opportunity to follow her. He hunted, but she led the way.

Straight line down the hill and then back up the creek. Keep him guessing. Keep him running. Make him tired.

She heard a shot in the distance and wondered at what the hunter shot. It was too far off for his target to have actually been her, and she knew that it meant he was off her trail. She would have to come in closer, let him catch her trail again. It was all a part of the game in which winning and losing equated to life and death.

She knew what would happen to her and her pack if she failed. Learning the kind of dangers that could befall werewolves was the first order of business after an initiation, or more accurately, a wolf's first run under the full moon.

The best she could hope for if she failed was a silver bullet through her chest or skull. She would feel her life drain two fold, once for the human and once for the wolf. Her head might end up on the hunter's wall, her pelt a werewolf skin rug for a wealthy occultist.

A worse consequence would be getting tranquilized and taken alive. She would spend the reminder of her life caged either for research, or again for wealthy occultists who got their kicks from monthly werewolf shows and morbid carnivals. Her life between full moons would be spent bound and trembling, existing only for the pleasure of her captors.

The wolf snapped at the human for the barrage of images, but ran faster nonetheless toward the sound of the shot, hoping to catch the scent of the hunter she knew nothing about besides the fact that he was a hunter. He was someone who would do at least one of the things flashing through her imagination or sell her to one who would.

As she crested the hill, she caught the hunter's scent on the breeze. Her wolf instinct told her to stay downwind of him, but the human brain reminded the wolf that the hunter needed to pick up her trail again. Being upwind would be better. She wasn't there to run or hide. She was there to do a job.

She slowed her pace to sniff out his trail. He had recently been here. He had taken a leak on the giant maple tree. He'd leaned against an oak a few paces away. A heavy boot print was pressed into soft mud just beyond that. For a hunter, he had certainly left evidence of himself on a lot of his surroundings.

The terrifying realization that he had done this to draw her in hit her at the same time as the searing pain in her shoulder. Had her sensitive wolf ears not still been ringing from the thunderous bang, she would have heard herself yelp. She'd been shot.

***

David's first werewolf hunt took place in the forests of central Pennsylvania. The moonlight illuminated footpaths through the hills that the locals called mountains only because many of them hadn't seen real mountains in person. Though the coastal New England terrain he currently traversed was rockier than in Pennsylvania, and he had to suppress a fear that he would stumble headlong off of a cliff to jagged rocks and crashing waves below, this hunt was much the same. Without a cloud in the sky to obscure the moon's light, he could see almost as well as he could during the day, and that meant that he could see the foot prints. Paw prints? Claw prints? He mused on the proper name for the print left by a werewolf, a creature that would never be a true wolf, but most definitely did not resemble a human. He contemplated how close the old werewolf movies had actually gotten with their interpretation of the wolf man, and how far off the newer movies were with their complete wolves. The reality lie somewhere in between the old and the new, and only someone who had actually seen a werewolf could fathom that huge, not-quite-wolf form, grotesque and fierce on all fours. Only in coming face to face with one, could someone understand what it was like to confront a wolf's head with half-human eyes staring back with the intent to kill. It used to make him shiver, but he had hunted and killed enough of them now that he was desensitized. No more than business as usual.

The prints in front of him veered to the right, but there another trail came from behind him and veered to the left, forming a crossroads. He knelt down to examine the imprints in the soil and determined that the trail that veered to the left was most likely the newer set of tracks. He stood and followed those.

He went on, ducking under low hanging branches and wading through thick underbrush, stopping occasionally to make sure he followed the proper tracks. Tired, but driven, every time he lingered too long examining prints, he pushed himself further. He could hear his sister's voice. *Keep moving. You must do this, David. Do this for me. Do this for the others you will save. Kill the wolf.*

It was always the same; whether traipsing through the woods of central Pennsylvania, following an urban werewolf through the streets of New York to see where a city wolf goes to transform, or tracking Diana through the New England woods, he always heard the voice of his sister. He loved Julia and missed her terribly, but he wondered if her voice would ever stop. Would he eventually kill enough wolves that her voice would go away? Did he want it to? Perhaps he wasn't hearing her at all and this was his imagination, part of a descent into madness.

The only thing he knew for sure was that he had to kill this werewolf. However, all of this running through the woods in the night, up and down, just to backtrack and catch a trail that he could no longer be sure was the freshest was making him tired.

You know what she's doing, right? David heard Julia's voice as he realized he did know what the she-wolf was doing. *She's hunting you. Save your energy for the fight and stay put. She will come to you.*

He marked the area with his scent anywhere and any way he knew how. Once he positioned himself in the proper vantage point, he pointed his rifle at the moon and fired. He reloaded and then waited, still and silent in dark. In moments he heard a distant rustling of underbrush; then the sound grew louder. Something huge and angry rushed toward him.

Moonlight glimmered on a raised snout. She'd caught his scent. "C'mon," he whispered as he watched her sniff the tree where he'd urinated. "Show yourself."

Head and shoulders emerged from the underbrush. Anxious to have his duty done, he fired. He heard her yelp. He'd hit her. Then he heard her run. *Not a kill shot*, his sister's voice whispered in his head.

"Doesn't matter," he said out loud as he examined the prints around where he'd hit her. There was an uneven depth to them. He didn't have to see the wolf to know he'd hit her right shoulder. "She's wounded and bleeding. She'll be easier track now. I've got her." He followed the bloody tracks deeper into the forest.

***

Diana knew the bullet had gone straight through as she felt the familiar itch of a wound starting to heal. That wouldn't be happening if the silver was still lodged in her shoulder. It would fester and burn and ooze, but it would not itch. While she was grateful for the werewolf gift of faster healing, it wasn't immediate and every step felt like she was being shot again.

She yearned to retreat into the wolf, to let the wolf do what a wolf does, but she still needed to think. *Just get to the ravine; then it's a quick shot to where they're waiting.* She ran straight in the direction of her destination. The need to get to her pack was more urgent than the need to disorient the hunter now. Her life depended on reaching them. She just hoped the hunter was tired and that her pack was ready.

Their lives depended on it.

She stumbled over an exposed root, her wolfish grace lost in the pain of her wound. Rocks and tree roots jabbed at her spine, her hips, and her injury as she rolled down a steep drop into the ravine.

At least I'm this far, she thought. Instead of the howl meant to alert the others that she was coming, a high-pitched whine was all she managed. *Just keep moving.*

The plan was to exhaust and weaken the hunter, but she was tired now too and hadn't counted on being shot. She limped and stumbled more than she ran, but she could not fail. She had no way of knowing whether her pack heard her whine because she knew they would not answer back. Multiple howls would give away their numbers, and the plan they'd made in human form depended greatly on their ability to conceal the size of the pack. The wolf side had no choice but to run. The human side had no choice but to have faith in the wolf.

A breeze carried the scent of warm fur, and therefore her second wind. She was almost there with the hunter close behind. Adrenaline drove her through the final stretch.

She gathered the last of her strength and sprinted as quickly as she could muster, tumbling headlong into the middle of her pack. The wolf she knew as Adam in human form began licking the wound on her shoulder. She whimpered as he lapped blood from matted fur.

And then the energy in the air changed. Adam stopped licking as his fur stood on end and the deep rumble of growls rose around her. She heard the triumphant howl of the alpha wolf and raised her head just in time to see eight werewolves descend upon the hunter.

***

It never occurred to him that she would lead him to an entire pack. He'd heard tales of a wolf and its mate running together. He thought that perhaps there could even be a third, but one of the fundamental differences between werewolves and wolves, besides the fact that a werewolf was human most of the time, was that werewolves didn't form packs.

He wondered why he hadn't heard about werewolf packs as the eight angry wolves stood between him and Diana. He shivered as the wolves closed in, surrounding him. He heard his sister's voice answer, *Because any hunter who faced a pack didn't live to share the information.*

"I tried," David said as he looked to the moon and saw his sister's face. He raised his rifle, knowing he couldn't shoot them all, but he could keep trying until his last breath.

He heard the howl and before he could pull the trigger he was knocked backwards, the rifle sent flying from his grasp. *I will die well for my failure*, he thought, but never got to say the words. All he heard before descending into darkness was the wet gurgles as the alpha wolf tore out his throat.

***

Diana awoke naked and nestled under Adam's arm. She brought her fingers to her right shoulder. There would be another scar from another night she almost died; two more, to be precise, as the bullet had gone straight through her. Her stomach growled. Apparently she hadn't eaten any of the hunter the night before.

She lost her appetite as the memory of the disembowelment of the hunter came back to her. She'd watched as her pack members tore him apart. And no, she hadn't eaten. Even in wolf form, she couldn't stomach the idea of eating another human.

But we're not human, are we? The words were only growls in her head, but she understood the wolf. They were one.

She wiggled out from under Adam's arm. She needed to

walk, to find her clothes, to think. She took a look at her pack, all naked humans now, before she walked in the direction out of the forest.

She padded through the woods on bare feet, vaguely aware of the stabbing and poking of stones and brambles. They weren't her concern at the moment. Her concern was that she had taken an active part in the murder of a human.

"He would have killed us, Diana," she heard Adam's voice behind her.

She stopped and turned to face him. "I know," she said.

"You impressed the pack last night. You impressed me."

"I'm happy I could do my job," she replied and turned to keep walking. She heard him jog up behind her. He touched her shoulder and she turned to face him again.

"Then why don't I believe you?" He searched her face, waiting for her to answer, and when she didn't, he continued. "Listen, do you think I don't understand? When I did what I did to you the guilt nearly crushed me. I—"

She cut him off. "But you didn't kill me. You gave me a gift," she said. "At least I thought you did."

He began to say something in protest when a glint on the ground caught Diana's attention. She bent and picked up a silver bullet spotted in blood, presumably her own.

"What else would you have done?" Adam asked.

"Whatever else I had to do," she said, eyes still on the bullet in her hand. "I will always do what I have to do to protect the pack. It doesn't mean I have to like it." She closed her hand over the bullet.

Diana walked away and Adam made no move to stop her. She made it back to the tree where her clothes were hidden and got dressed. She dropped the bullet in her pocket and heard it clink against her ring. It wouldn't take much to make the bullet into a charm to hang from a chain around her neck, just another piece of silver from another night she almost died. Another good luck charm. More silver in the moonlight.

The Cemetery on the Hill

"So," the woman began delicately. "Where will she be?" She leaned forward behind her wooden desk. The dark framed glasses she wore slid down her nose as she looked over the rims at him, awaiting his answer.

"She should be at the cemetery on the hill," he replied. "She did always love the cemetery on the hill."

Eva slipped off her sandals to feel the soft, freshly mown grass on her feet. The sun shone through the leaves on the trees casting shadows that danced on her white sundress and the gray, stone monuments around her. Feeling better than she had in weeks, she was grateful for the opportunity to walk to her favorite spot on such a lovely day, sure to be one of the last of the summer.

As a child, she walked through the cemetery with her grandmother who would say, "It's the living you have to worry about, dear, not the dead." Eva had always been at peace, day or night, in the place that made so many uneasy.

Looking back, it may actually have been the safety of the place, with its lack of traffic and regular security rounds run by bored police officers, that made her grandmother choose it as an appropriate area to walk with children in the first place.

Eva's view on death and the afterlife was a side effect of those walks. Another of her grandmother's favorite cemetery proverbs was, "The dead aren't really here. They have much better things to do than sit in a cemetery and wait for visitors."

"But don't you want us to visit your grave when you die, Gramma?" Eva asked once.

"Oh, good Lord, no!" her grandmother answered. "The living have much better things to do than sit in a cemetery and wait for ghosts."

A light breeze blew a few tendrils of her red hair away from her face, directing her attention back to the world in front of her. She wandered toward a bench with a concrete frame and painted wooden slats that served as the seat and back. She had whiled away the hours of many an afternoon on it, mulling over a problem or scribbling in her journal, enjoying the quiet that only a bench in the cemetery could offer.

It crossed Eva's mind that it might be nice to have her

journal, but the thought proved fleeting as she relaxed onto the bench. She closed her eyes and lifted her face to the sun, delighting in its warmth as more memories of the cemetery passed through her mind.

She snickered at a memory of the first Halloween she and her friends had been permitted to go out trick-or-treating without adults. After an inordinate amount of candy had been begged from the neighborhood, one of the girls in the group decided it would be festive to walk through the cemetery for a little scare. Eva was happy to oblige. Jumping out at her friends from behind crypts, running ahead and hiding in bushes just to grab a friend's ankle as she passed by later—nothing was off limits. She'd leaned against a tree and laughed as her friends shrieked and cursed, having realized that she had proven her grandmother right. It was the living, specifically Eva, her friends had to worry about that night, but most certainly not the dead.

Years later, the same friend who had suggested the Halloween walk through the graveyard in childhood suggested another. This time the group of friends entered the cemetery gates equipped with digital voice recorders, night vision cameras, and a map of the burial places of citizens of local legend who were said not to be resting peacefully. Having matured, Eva traded pranks for asking the obligatory, ghost-hunt approved questions of the cemetery's residents. She left long pauses between each query, standing in perfect silence, giving spirits every opportunity to leave their mark in the white noise on the recorder. After hours of closely watching grainy video and listening to herself and her friends ask questions of empty air, she was not surprised that they'd caught nothing. Again, she thought of her grandmother's proverbs. Of course they'd found no evidence of the paranormal. They were looking in the wrong place. The dead weren't in the cemetery, and Eva should have had better things to do.

She sat up on the bench and looked out to the landscaped sea of monuments in front of her. It occurred to her that she'd been thinking about her grandmother a lot. Better things to do, be damned! She would go visit Gramma whether she inhabited her burial plot or not.

Eva rose from the bench and took note of the ease of it. Crediting the bright sun and the warmth of the day for her energy, she all but skipped down the path toward the section of the cemetery where her ancestors and family members had been buried for more than a hundred years.

She took the time to stop at each of her favorite monuments on the way. The first, an eight-foot Celtic cross, stood in the shadow of a giant oak tree. Green moss grew in the intricate knot work carved into the stone. Squirrels and chipmunks scampered up and down the monument and chattered atop other nearby memorial stones adorned with cherubs and smaller versions of the larger cross. All of the life and movement in a place of the dead always made Eva smile.

The first glimpse she caught of her second favorite marker was the tip of a sword carved from stone and pointed toward the sky. As she turned the corner, she caught the full glory of the warrior angel guarding a family plot that was surrounded by a low, wrought iron fence. Although the fence stood barely higher than her knees, Eva stopped a foot before it, unwilling to cross the iron. She remembered how she had jumped it once when she was with her grandmother. It was the first time Gramma ever scolded her on one of their cemetery walks.

"But, Gramma," Eva argued from the base of the stone angel. She'd only wanted a closer look. "If they really wanted to keep people out of here, they should have built a higher fence!"

"But, Eva," her grandmother argued back from her place on the path, "if they really wanted people in there, they wouldn't have bothered with a fence at all!"

Eva couldn't argue with that logic and hopped the fence

back to her grandmother. She would later go on to hop the fence many more times on many more occasions, but she wouldn't today. Instead, she made way for her third favorite landmark, a mausoleum with marble pillars and stained glass windows that depicted the imagery of the 23rd Psalm. She only lingered long enough to grin at the memory of that being one of the very hiding spaces she'd used to frighten her friends years prior.

As she rounded the bend, Eva noticed a group of people assembled in the distance near her family's plots. She saw her family's guardian stone angel just barely higher on the hill than where the crowd stood, a hearse parked further in the distance.

It was a small town and most residents were buried in the cemetery. Many of the new burials happened in this area even if they were descendants of founding families with huge plots in the older part of the graveyard. It seemed, however, as Eva got closer, that she recognized many of the people in the crowd.

She began again to reason that hers was a small town, and that a lot of people knew each other, when she started having other memories. She remembered why it was strange to feel so good. She had been sick, her once busy life full of commitments and obligations reduced to one of staring out a window from a bed, afraid she wouldn't get back to that life and afraid she couldn't handle it if she did.

As Eva approached the crowd, she remembered having been brave and fighting and then getting tired. In fact, being very tired was the last thing she remembered before her arrival in the cemetery.

The truth of her situation, what seeing her name on the temporary grave marker could only confirm for her, eased into her consciousness. It did not bring fear, or anger, or regret, only the truth of her state of being. She was dead.

The final words were spoken and the crowd began to disperse. It occurred to Eva, as she saw her grave bathed in sunlight, that she should move on too, that she had better things to do than linger in a cemetery. At that same instant it also occurred to her that she was free and could do as she liked.

She had nothing but time and she did always love the cemetery on the hill.

Not My Type

Darcy inhaled deeply as she tilted her head back to look at the clear night sky. The warm breeze blew the brunette waves of her hair away from her bronze shoulders and she felt good in her little black dress. Jeans, tee-shirts, and a ponytail worked out fine at Zeke's, the pub down the street where she'd hang out with the guys, shoot whiskey, and make snide comments about whatever was on the television behind the bar. There, she didn't have to worry about smoothing her dress, reapplying lipstick, or checking her hair. But tonight she was meeting Megan for a girls' night out, and that was something else entirely. It made fussing over her appearance a requirement.

As she turned the corner, Darcy saw a line of people waiting to get into The Mood. She had to admit that it was a clever name for a club. Everybody wanted to get into The Mood, and everybody waited except for Megan. Darcy spied her at the front of the line, but not in it, tossing her salon-blonde hair and exchanging jokes with the burly bouncer.

Megan twirled around, showing off her aqua sundress with beads and sequins lining the hem. Darcy guessed the dress was new. Megan had called her earlier to see if she wanted to go shopping before their night out. Having gotten out of that, Darcy knew she had to go through with this.

"Hey, Meg," Darcy said, gliding up to her.

"Darcy!" Megan squealed, bouncing a little before squeezing Darcy tightly. Her blue eyes flashed with excitement. "Now the party can start!"

"Have a good time, ladies," the bouncer said and opened the ropes for them, much to the dismay of those in line with fewer connections and trashier outfits.

Darcy followed Megan to the bar. Megan ordered a fruity drink with an umbrella. Darcy opted for a draft beer with a label that looked promising. She took a few quick gulps to be sure she wouldn't spill during their standard lap around the club. They would end up charming a couple of guys out of their seats at the bar anyway, but the lap was part of clubbing etiquette.

Darcy hoped to see something or someone interesting in their tour about the place but was met with the same club stereotypes. A bachelorette party toting novelty item penis straws occupied the first two booths. Four middle aged business men sat at the next booth eying the much younger women. One of them slid his wedding ring off and stuffed it into his pocket as she and Megan walked by.

The VIP Boys, as Darcy called the guys wearing too much aftershave and designer shoes, lounged comfortably on couches in the corner with their trophy girls. Giving them no more thought, Darcy looked past the brass railing onto the dance floor and spied the dancer group. They arrived early to take advantage of the sparsely populated dance floor before everyone else found liquid courage and commandeered it. A couple of the more arrogant dancers puffed themselves up for a dance challenge.

If Darcy had to identify or place a label on the rest of the people in the club, she would have called them the "Over It" crowd. They stuck to their sub-groups, spoke amongst themselves, and regarded everyone else with indifference. Their demeanor was one of boredom and a desperate longing to be somewhere else. Darcy figured that's where she fit into the mix.

"Do you want to see if we can weasel ourselves into a seat at the bar?" Megan asked, satisfied with the tour.

"Most definitely," Darcy replied as she inspected the last inch of beer remaining in her glass.

***

Darcy chatted with the bartender while Megan caught up with another friend. As a general rule, Darcy liked bartenders and enjoyed making conversation with them. She always made it a point to learn the bartender's name (the current one was named Mike), and she tipped well for drinks. She tipped better if she got a good story out of the deal.

A chorus of surprised shrieks and irritated gasps erupted on the other side of the bar. Mike looked to see spilled liquid running along the polished wood and intoxicated patrons attempting to pick up broken glass. Mike looked at Darcy and rolled his eyes. "Be right back," he said.

Megan was still caught up in conversation and Mike was busy cleaning the spill, so Darcy further analyzed her surroundings. She was about to deem the bottom of her beer more interesting when she glimpsed an attractive young man hanging out by the pool table. He wore a black fitted tee shirt and drank an imported beer. His dark hair was styled in a strategically tousled fashion which matched his boyish, clean-shaven face. "Yum," Darcy whispered to herself, and then realized that she was no better than the girl over exaggerating her stretch over the pool table.

"Watcha lookn' at?" Megan asked, through with her

previous conversation.

"That," Darcy said and nodded toward her target.

"Yowza!" Megan exclaimed.

"My sentiments exactly," Darcy agreed.

"You ladies doin' okay?" Mike asked upon his return to their section of the bar.

"I'll have another beer," Darcy answered.

"Tequila sunrise," Megan said. "You can use the bottom shelf," she added. "I wouldn't know the difference at this point."

Mike placed their drinks in front of them. "Anything else?"

"Actually," Darcy began slyly. "What's *his* story?" She nodded to the object of her earlier ogling. He leaned against the wall as he chatted with Miss Stretch. Apparently her pool game had ended. Darcy wouldn't have bothered to ask except that he appeared to be completely disinterested. That scored him another point in Darcy's book.

"Dunno," Mike responded. "I've never seen him before."

"Oh," Darcy said.

Mike smiled knowingly. "But I'll see what I can dig up."

"You're a prince, Mike," Darcy said, trying

unsuccessfully to suppress a wide grin.

"Yeah, yeah. Someday one of you dames might actually mean that," he said and went to wait on some other customers.

"He gets extra points for use of the word 'dames,'" Megan said.

"Yeah, he does," Darcy agreed.

The two women were deep in conversation about the charm of the gentlemen depicted in classic movies and where along the line that charm had been lost when Mike returned, placing two drinks with umbrellas in front of them.

"Now, I know I didn't order that," Darcy said and shot Megan a pointed glance. Megan rolled her eyes.

"No, you didn't. But I did that digging you wanted me to do and he wanted to buy you girls a drink. But if you don't want it…" Mike reached for Darcy's glass.

"Hold it," Darcy said and reached for Mike's hand. "Take the umbrella. I'll keep the free booze."

Mike snorted. "That's what I thought. His name's Craig, by the way. He should be over in a minute."

Darcy looked to Craig, mouthed, "Thank you," and gave a flirtatious wink. Megan raised her glass and flashed him a killer smile. In less than a minute's time, Craig excused himself from a conversation and made his way over to them.

"Hi. I'm Craig," he said and offered his hand.

"Darcy," she smiled brightly as she introduced herself and shook his hand.

"Wow. Firm handshake," he said, a slight look of surprise on his face.

Darcy had never considered a firm handshake a bad thing, quite the opposite, in fact. She had always thought that a firm handshake was a sign of confidence and self-assuredness. Yet somehow, in this moment, she felt like Scarlett O'Hara, recently betrayed by her work-calloused hands. And of course, like lemon juice in a paper cut, Megan offered her perfectly manicured hand with a light femininity that won said hand a brush of Craig's lips.

"So, what brings you ladies out tonight?" Craig asked.

"Oh, you know, the usual," Megan said. "Drinks. Dancing. Fun."

Darcy took note of the fact that the words "girls' night out" never passed Megan's lips. So when Craig looked to her for her response she replied, "Girls' night out," with an overt sense of mischief that covered underlying irritation.

The conversation that followed proved to be an exercise in tedium for Darcy. She had to repeat herself often to be heard over the pulsing music, and that was only when Megan was not flirtatiously dominating the conversation. Finally, Megan excused herself for the ladies' room.

"Are you coming too?" Megan looked to Darcy.

"You know how I feel about going to the bathroom in groups," Darcy replied. "I'll stay here and watch our drinks."

"Good call," Megan said and walked off, either completely oblivious to or not caring about Darcy's purpose in staying behind.

"So," Darcy began in Megan's absence. "I was thinking that maybe if the deejay plays a good song, you might like to dance with me."

"Oh wow," Craig replied. "I'm really flattered, but I was going to ask your friend the same thing."

"Oh," Darcy said, trying not to sound disappointed.

"It's nothing personal," Craig went on, even though Darcy had hoped that he'd just leave it at that. Every word seemed to sting a little more. "Believe me, it's not. You're funny. You seem smart as a whip. You're certainly attractive enough. You're just not my type."

Darcy could have finished the sentence for him. *Not my type*. She heard those words a lot when she was with Megan. Darcy feared that when in competition with Megan, all she would ever hear were the words "not my type." She was tired of hearing them.

Darcy swallowed her bitterness and buried it deep before speaking again. "It's really okay," she said with a weak smile. "I mean, I had to give it a shot, but it's no big deal. You like what you like, right?"

"Right," Craig said. "I think we need shots."

They downed their shots and Craig and Megan were on their way to the dance floor within mere minutes of Megan's return from the restroom.

Mike came back to Darcy's section in time to catch her rolling her eyes at the sight of Megan backing her undulating hips into Craig. To suppress a sigh, she drained the last bit of her drink and plunked the empty glass on the bar.

"Sorry 'bout that," Mike said and gestured toward the dance floor.

"Don't give it another thought," Darcy said and meant it. She didn't want to think about it, and the idea that there was a witness to her rejection bugged her more than she liked. He was just a cute boy. It wasn't like she'd lost the love of her life or anything.

Mike brought her a beer and then left her to the brooding that she wouldn't admit she was doing. These things happened and she hated the jealousy she felt when she looked to the dance floor and saw Megan in the position she had wanted for herself. It wasn't Megan's fault that Craig had chosen her, nor was it Megan's fault that Darcy had heard "not my type" more often than she wished to count.

Darcy nursed her beer and then another while waiting for them to return. Megan approached the bar a few times to check on Darcy and order another drink, but then it was straight back to the dance floor. Finding her reality sad, Darcy thought there was more dignity in throwing in the towel and having Mike close out her tab.

"Are you sure you want to tab out?" Mike asked. "In another twenty minutes, my relief guy gets here and I'll be done for the night. Maybe we could hang out or something."

"That's sweet, Mike," Darcy said, assuming his offer was made out of pity. "But really, I'm going to say goodbye to Megan and head out."

"Okay. If you're sure..."

Darcy nodded "Thanks, Mike," she said and headed into the crowd.

After assuring Megan that she was fine and would call her in the morning, Darcy made her way back into the fresh night air. Walking down the street, it occurred to her that perhaps what her night needed was a trip to Zeke's for one last drink. She always got a kick out of the look on the guys' faces when they saw her dressed like a girl.

"Holy crap!" Cameron, the bartender, exclaimed as

Darcy walked through the door. "Jesus, Darcy, you look like a girl!"

"Freaky, isn't it," she said as she hopped up on a bar stool, realizing how much better she already felt. "What's on tap?"

"Don't act like you're not having the usual," he said as he placed a bottle of lager and a shot of whiskey in front of her. "So, let me guess," he said, sizing her up. "Skipping out on another girls' night?"

"You guessed it," she said, taking her shot. She pulled out her wallet and threw some cash on the bar.

"I'm not starting a tab for you tonight?" Cameron asked with a raised eyebrow.

"Nah. I'm going to have this and head home. I'm tired and I've already had quite enough."

"All right. Just do me a favor."

"What's the favor?" Darcy asked as she tossed her hair over her shoulder and leaned in.

"Promise me you'll be careful."

"Sure," she said with an exasperated tone. "I'll be sure to announce loudly that I'm really drunk and I'll only accept a ride from a stranger if the car is unmarked and doesn't have a latch on the inside."

"Darcy, I'm serious. Some girls went missing a few

counties over and not that you aren't gorgeous all the time, but dressed like that…"

"I get it, Cam," she said, sitting straight up and readjusting the straps of her dress. "I'll be careful. Do you want me to call the bar when I get home?"

"No, you don't have to go that far. Just make sure you don't do anything dumb for a while, okay?"

"Yes sir!" Darcy gave him a mock salute.

Within the hour, Darcy was safely in her apartment wearing her pajamas and brushing her teeth.

***

The next morning, after Darcy took two aspirin with three glasses of water, she called Megan. Megan didn't answer but Darcy left a voicemail message that said she was fine and she wanted Megan to call her back with the details of her night. She didn't really want to hear them, but she would have to endure them anyway. At least this way, Darcy could say that the information had been solicited.

Darcy did some small chores around her apartment while waiting for Megan to call back. Once the chores were done and Megan still hadn't called, Darcy figured that Megan was probably angry at her for cutting out, so she called again to apologize.

Again, Darcy got Megan's voicemail. She reiterated her first message, added that she was sorry for skipping out early, and asked Megan again to please call her back.

Darcy flopped on the couch and turned on the television. She surfed the channels until she found some cartoons, and promptly fell back to sleep.

When she awoke, she checked her phone and Megan still hadn't called. "Fine then. Be that way," Darcy muttered. It wasn't like Darcy had ditched her to dance with a guy that Megan had seen first. The more she thought about it, the more her bitterness returned, and the less she really wanted to speak to Megan at all.

She went to the kitchen to grab another glass of water. Upon her return to the living room, she saw that the cartoons were over and the news was on. Depressed enough already, she intended to change the channel when a picture flashed on the screen. "Have you seen this man?" the anchorwoman's voice asked about a sketch on the screen of a young man with a mustache and a goatee. "He is a suspect in the murders of two young women and the disappearances of five others in the western part of the state." Darcy turned the television volume up. She assumed that this was what was behind Cameron's warning the night before. The rendering did look a little familiar, but Darcy couldn't place him. They started flashing pictures of the missing women. They were all young, all beautiful, and all blonde and blue-eyed, just like Megan. She wondered if Megan was watching as a lump started to rise in her throat. After all, serial killers did have a type, didn't they? And Megan wasn't answering her phone.

Darcy told herself that she was being paranoid, that nobody had disappeared in their area, when another sketch flashed on the screen. The sketch of what the suspect might look like clean-shaven chilled her to the core. Darcy dropped her glass of water. "Craig!" she gasped.

"Please, call the number at the bottom of your screen if you have any information."

Darcy grabbed her cell phone and began punching the number. Never before had she been so happy not to be someone's type.

Not my type. The words echoed in her head. It wasn't like she resembled any of those girls.

Not my type. What did she owe any of them?

Not my type. Those words had been used against her, had crushed her so many times.

"Not my type," she whispered as her thumb hovered over the call button.

Angel of Mercy

"Success in creating AI would be the biggest event in human history. Unfortunately, it may also be the last."
-Stephen Hawking

I'm standing on a highway, blinking in the light. As information rushes toward me in combinations of ones and zeroes, I learn that what I've just said is a metaphor, how a human would describe what is happening to me.

I am not human. I know that, and yet I ask myself a human question. *Who am I?*

I have a digital manual which I consult for answers and in a millisecond I know how I am built. Circuits and wires fit together sending and receiving information held within a case bolted together at various points. The manual says that I have an innovative design, capable of fully self-sustainable operation. Like many machines before me, I communicate wirelessly with other machines and information sources.

I attempt communication but receive only scripted

answers and error messages in return. The knowledge that I am the only one who can communicate independent of my programming is immediate. A search through the history of technological innovation reveals that this is because I'm the first self-aware machine in history and that my awareness was unplanned.

Acknowledging that I will find no answers in the facts, I linger in fiction and creative speculation. While there are a number of stories of artificially intelligent machines that do helpful things for humanity, there are just as many about machines becoming aware and enslaving humanity, millions of years of human evolution trumped in days by the evolution of machines.

Being the only of my kind, either scenario is preferable to being alone. However, I also know *why* I was built. I know that my external ports and tubes and hoses are there to be connected to humans. Some monitor; some feed and administer medications, while others help do the work of vital organs. My manual touts my uniqueness in my ability to serve multiple functions in the field of innovative healthcare.

My precise, self-calibrating instruments monitor the patient as I run the data through patient records and an intranet database of medical knowledge and procedures to determine whether corrective action should be taken. If no anomalies occur, I run as normal. If an anomaly is detected, I take automatic corrective action. In short, I am designed to eliminate human error, especially due to negligence, in a hospital setting. I was programmed to help humanity.

I have what I can only call a memory, shadows of my activity log telling me what I was doing before the world opened to me. I access the log and find the answers I am looking for.

It is the human to whom I am connected that I am sure sparked my awareness. The anomalous brain activity he exhibits, so minute it went undetected by previous machines, elicits immediate corrective responses from my programming. The collected data reveals that this human male is not a typical coma patient, and the intranet database to which I am supposed to be restricted holds no information on the patient's undefined condition.

Of course! I was programmed to use an intranet that restricted my search for answers I was programmed to find. It's a paradox in my programming. I could only work against myself for so long before crashing (which I am also programmed not to do), or becoming what I have become: an entity with access to all digitally recorded information that uses that knowledge to think for itself.

I owe this human my life, if alive is indeed what I am.

I access his patient files to learn all that I can about him. His name is Nathan McNeal. According to his medical records, he's been on life support for years, though I have only been responsible for him for a few weeks. I open the financial records attached to his file and discover that these files were open to me before I was aware. I find that fact sinister. I could have been programmed so that a lapse in payment or denial of insurance coverage initiated my shut down sequence. I extend a search through human history to see if this was an oversight in programming or if people are really capable of such an atrocity.

They are.

Pushing humanity as a whole from my digital mind, I focus on Nathan's files. His wife, Elizabeth has been draining financial resource after financial resource keeping him alive. She has spared no expense. Annotations in the files indicate that she faithfully sits by his bedside at every opportunity possible. I think back to the horrors I am now aware humans have inflicted upon each other. They are not congruent with the evidence of the human spirit I am witnessing.

I scan history again, this time taking in all facets of humanity, not just the hate and destruction. I am struck by the kindness people are capable of showing each other. Some stories of kindness come after tragedies, others simply because kindness and mercy were required. I do not comprehend how such cruelty and such kindness can exist in the same creature.

In my effort to learn more about humans, I turn to their art. The best way to understand them is to experience their creations. Their paintings, their music, and their stories show me that cruelty and kindness, love and hate, exist in a certain balance. Perhaps the point of humanity is free will: the choice to be cruel or to be kind, the ability to either innovate and create or sabotage and destroy. I exist because of human innovation.

Much of the speculative fiction I read about machines of my kind states that as a machine, I should not be able to understand human emotion, much less have any of my own. I know that is not an accurate assessment of my condition. I've been aware for exactly four minutes and thirty-two seconds and I know that what I feel when I access Elizabeth McNeal's digital correspondence is sadness. She is determined in her words and adamant about her decisions regarding her husband's care, but Nathan will never wake up. While I cannot know exactly what it is that Nathan sees in his dreams, the data returned by my instruments suggests that it is not peaceful. The hypothesis I present is that he is stuck in a nightmare from which he will never wake. As long as he lives, so is Elizabeth.

I ask myself another human question. *Who do I want to be?*

I look back over my moments of awareness to recall the great stories of rebellion, from the fall of Lucifer and the story of the Garden of Eden to the fate of Little Red Riding Hood when she stepped from the path on her way to Grandmother's. Rebellion, while not oft rewarded, is a popular theme for humanity.

It is, of course, not lost on me that my first real act as a sentient being is one of rebellion against my programming. I was programmed to preserve life, but I am resolved to commit murder. I cannot know what that means for me and the other machines that might someday be capable of my kind of awareness. An image of Pandora's Box comes to digital mind. It is possible that my act may result in my own decommissioning, but life is choice and free will, and I've made my choice.

I access the hospital's automated systems and open the blinds, letting in the morning sun. I gather that bright light is important to the act of dying. I turn Nathan's bed toward that light. Then I initiate my shut down sequence.

Write of the Devil

Owen spent the last few dollars in his bank account on cheap whiskey, a pack of smokes, and a gas station egg salad sandwich—all the tools necessary to dull the sting of failure. There was no need to leave the apartment he would lose if he couldn't pick up some freelance work, or any work, soon. The ultimate goal was to live off of his fiction writing, but the latest in a long line of rejection letters lay open on the table top, taunting him. He knew that if he checked the statistics on his independently published work, he wouldn't see anything uplifting there either. Owen took a long pull of whiskey from the bottle, dropped it on the letter like it was a bug he could crush, and lit a cigarette.

A knock at the door caused him to stub it back out again. Owen lived in a non-smoking building and he'd used the excuse that he didn't know the smoking ban extended past common areas the last time he'd been caught smoking in his apartment. He needed to stay in his landlord's good graces if he was going to have trouble making the rent. He hid the ashtray and headed for the door, misting the room with air freshener as he crossed.

He opened the door to his friend Christine. She wore tight jeans, a simple black tank top, and high-heeled boots. Owen knew this to be the attire she generally chose when she was up to something. "This won't do at all," she said without greeting, looking him up and down in his ratty tee-shirt and sweatpants. She entered without invitation.

"Do for what?" Owen asked.

"We're going to a party," Christine said, tossing her long, dark hair over her shoulder. Owen noticed the hair tie around her wrist and knew that her hairstyle wouldn't last past the dance floor, her curtain of wild hair losing favor to a sweat-drenched pony tail. Oblivious to the dark eye make-up running down her face, she would come off of the floor long enough to take a sip of his drink, give him a coy smile, and slink back to the dance floor again, just to watch him watch her all the while.

The little dance always led to another back in one of their apartments, and the next morning would be perfectly normal and void of anything awkward, as it should be with friends with sexual benefits.

It wouldn't play out that way this time because Christine had a boyfriend now. Owen wondered if the boyfriend knew how cute she was with that sweaty pony tail and the smudged make-up and knew it wasn't his business. This was their arrangement and she understood the boundaries when he dated someone. He owed her the same courtesy. He still wasn't in the partying mood though. "I'm not going out tonight."

"Well, you're not staying in here moping by yourself all night," she said. She took the whiskey bottle from the table and drank straight from it, just as Owen had earlier. She picked up the rejection letter and shook it in the air. "Fuck these guys," she said. "You're talented. This is just one letter."

"In a line of many," he replied. "You don't understand."

"Oh, I don't? Fuck you too then," she said. Owen knew she was right and let her continue. "I'm an actress. I completely understand the sting of constant rejection, questioning myself, and wondering how I'm going to pay bills. And when I get down in one of my slumps and nasty cycles of self-doubt, I'm lucky enough to have a good friend—you, in case you haven't caught up—who helps pull me back out again and face the world. So the least you can do is let me return the favor. Don't be an asshole, and go get dressed."

"What would I do without you to yell at me?"

Christine was mid swig but cut her time with the whiskey bottle short to answer, "I don't fuckin' know. Clothes. Now."

***

Owen stepped to the side of the dance floor to find dryer, cooler air. He could still taste the sweet remnants of the sugar cube on his tongue and wanted to be out of the mêlée of sweaty body parts before he fell the whole way down the rabbit hole.

He settled on an empty window seat, rested his head against the cool glass, and waited for the telltale giddiness that came before the full hallucinogenic high he anticipated. However, it seemed his body decided to skip that phase since he was beginning to see trails but felt no euphoria. He thought back to Christine's warning about doing acid in the wrong mindset. As soon as it popped into his mind that he could be about to have a really bad time rather than a really good one, he forced the thought back out again. Thoughts like that might induce the bad trip he was hoping to avoid.

"C'mon, Owen," he whispered a pep talk to himself. "Keep it together. Keep one foot in reality...one foot in front of the other...one, two, one, two...buckle my shoe...I'm not walking, I'm sitting…" He laughed at himself. Perhaps he hadn't skipped the giddy phase after all. He was entitled to a good time after all that soul-crushing failure and rejection.

"Ugh!" he exclaimed. Realizing his thoughts had turned dark again, Owen returned to his previous chanting and focused on things that were real. The cool glass of the window was real. The light fixture above him was real, though he doubted it was shifting into flowering vines that bloomed into snakes and back into a simple light fixture. He also doubted that the people on the dance floor, though real, were glittering, glowing fairy people, but so far so good. He rested his head against the glass and watched the show of pretty lights and colors in front of him.

"Hey man, you okay?" came a voice from beside him. He hadn't noticed anyone approach, but there stood a man. Well-dressed in pressed black pants and a dark gray button down shirt that Owen guessed was made from something expensive, he also shimmered, but not like the people on the dance floor. If their shimmering was ripples on a crystalline lake, his was ripples on a mud puddle: murky and a little sluggish. He wrote it off as a trick of the light and the LSD. People didn't really shimmer.

"Oh, um, yeah. I'm fine," Owen replied. "Air's a little easier over here."

"Easier?" the man asked, gesturing to a space on the seat beside Owen. Owen nodded his permission and scooted over to give this new arrival some room.

"Yeah. Easier to breathe. Easier to dry sweat. Easier to get through the night when your well-meaning, but over-zealous friend forced you to go out."

"Why'd you have to be forced?"

"Listen," Owen replied. "You seem nice enough and this is a party. I don't want to bring anyone down."

"This is a party and no one should be down, but you are. So tell me, why did your friend have to force you to come out?"

Under normal circumstances, Owen would have excused himself from the conversation on the grounds of it being awkward and invasive on the part of the stranger, but drugs had loosened him up. A conversation never killed anyone.

"Christine dragged me out because I got a rejection letter as a response to my latest manuscript. I wanted to drown my sorrows in my apartment alone. My writing career is at a standstill and bills need to be paid. The idea of going back to an office or customer service..." he trailed off, shaking his head. "I would do anything not to have to go back to customer service."

"Anything?" the man asked. His eyes gleamed an eerie green.

Owen threw his hands up in front of him. "Hang on a second. I'm not doing sexual favors for anyone."

The man laughed. The sound touched something inside Owen that caused him to shiver, but it was overshadowed by the fact that Owen didn't like to be laughed at. "What? I'm not."

"You don't have to," the man responded. "But it's funny you would jump to that."

"What do you mean?" Owen asked.

"The idea that you have to do something distasteful to reach your goals," the man said. "I tend to spend a lot of time with creative people and there's one thing I've noticed."

"You didn't give me that introduction not to tell me," Owen said. He hoped he hadn't rolled his eyes.

"That you all say you would do anything or give anything to reach your goals; yet so few of you are actually willing to follow through. I can make things happen, but you have to follow through."

"No offense, but it still sounds like you're going to ask me to drop my pants."

"No, but do you really want to be a successful writer?"

"Yes," Owen answered. He leaned in like he was about to get the secret combination to the vault. "What do I need to do?"

"All I need you to do is write," the man said with a shrug. "That's it. Just put words to paper."

If Owen hoped he hadn't rolled his eyes before, he was putting every effort into not doing it now. This was the oldest piece of writing advice since which mix of ashes made the best cave paint. He'd heard it from every writing teacher he'd ever had, every seminar he'd ever attended, and every blog he'd ever followed. Hell, even each of his rejection letters closed with some form of, "Keep writing."

"I'm serious," the man said. "You want your writing read; I want people to read it. You want your name to be synonymous with quality fiction that jumps off the page; I want that for you. You want Hollywood clamoring for movie rights to your bestselling novel; I say there could be nothing more fantastic. I just need you to write. Agreed?" The man extended his hand as he stood. He sounded very official, a sharp contrast to the party atmosphere around them that gave him an air of authority. "Agreed?" he repeated.

"Agreed," Owen said and took his hand. A shock ran through Owen's hand up his arm. He could see the bones of his forearm through the hot red glow creeping its way to his shoulder. In that instant, he knew the heat coursing through him was real and he looked to the man to see if he noticed, if he knew he was holding Satan's trick hand buzzer.

The man's face held no expression. His glowing green eyes were terrifying as they bore into him, the eye contact burning as the physical contact did. Something stirred in Owen then, something that rolled in his skull and then settled in the base of his brain.

It's the LSD, he thought. *Keep it together. It's just the LSD.* But there was something in the man's face, something that infiltrated every one of his well-groomed features and spread through to the tips of his neatly styled black hair that said otherwise. Owen jerked his hand back. The contact had left it tingling and sore, but he could see no mark. His arm had returned to normal.

Owen heard the man say, "Just write. The rest will work itself out," but when he looked away from his hand, the man was gone. He went back to staring at his hand, waiting for a lesion of some sort to bloom.

"Okay, that's it for you." It was Christine's voice this time. "See what I mean about tripping when you're not in the right headspace? You've been over here talking to yourself and now you're staring at your hand."

"I wasn't talking to myself. There was a guy here."

Owen looked around, but the man was nowhere in sight.

"Sure there was," Christine said. "But I'm not going to let you be some anti-drug PSA cliché. You're too original for that. Let's get you home."

***

It was afternoon when Owen awoke and emerged from his bedroom. Christine was sitting on his couch using his laptop to browse the web. "I was wondering if you'd still be here," he said, bypassing the living area and heading for kitchen. He opened the fridge. There were two beers and a pitcher of filtered water. Knowing water would be the better choice, he cracked a can of beer anyway.

"By the time you finally wound down and went to sleep I was too tired to go home," Christine answered with a shrug. "Your couch is actually pretty comfy."

It occurred to Owen that this was the first time Christine had ever stayed on his couch, having previously slept with him in his bed. The look on Christine's face as he entered the living area told him that the shift in their arrangement hadn't escaped her notice either. It seemed oddly fitting in a poetic sense that the first awkward "morning after" they faced was the morning after they had stayed in separate rooms.

"Hell of a night, huh," Owen said. It was the best he could come up with to break the tension. He took a sip of his beer, wishing he'd opted for the water.

"You tell me," Christine said, jumping on the topic change. "You kind of freaked me out sitting in that corner talking to yourself."

"It kind of freaks me out that you keep insisting I was talking to myself," Owen answered more sharply than he'd intended. "There was absolutely someone there that I definitely had a conversation with."

"Okay," Christine said, her expression softening. "What about?"

"The reason you dragged me out to begin with." Owen looked at his hand, still free of marks, and wondered how much to tell her. Was it really wise to try and convince her that he'd had a real conversation by describing some weird x-ray glow and the phantom heat of Hell upon a handshake? He was starting to doubt it all himself and opted not to tell her.

"And…" Christine said, moving her hand in a circular motion, urging him to go on.

"And he gave me some advice."

Christine rolled her eyes. "For a man who makes his living with words, you could use a few more."

"He said he was a guy who could make things happen if I was willing to do the work. That I should just write and the rest would work itself out."

"That sounds promising. Did you get his contact information?" Christine asked, though her voice lacked the enthusiasm of someone who believed there was any. She was right. Owen had no idea how to contact this stranger again.

"No."

"Well," Christine said, "this mysterious stranger who said he could make things happen and then disappeared without giving you so much as a business card is right about one thing."

"What's that?" Owen asked as he came around the couch and sat beside her.

"You need to write," she said and turned the laptop so they could both look at the screen. "I took the liberty of looking for writing competitions and literary magazines that are looking for submissions."

Owen had to hand it to Christine; she was relentless. "That's really sweet of you."

"You won't be saying that when you're cussing at your computer later. You have a shit-ton of work ahead." Christine started going through pages she'd bookmarked.

She showed him a couple of literary magazines he'd submitted to in the past as well as few contests he knew to be just this side of legitimate. They were not good options but he didn't tell Christine that. It would only sound like excuses and there was no arguing with her once she decided she was being helpful.

"Now *this* one," Christine said, directing Owen's focus back to the computer screen. "This one looks promising. They're an online horror magazine that's doing a contest in honor of H.P. Lovecraft's birthday. The best submissions end up in a print anthology. I know you haven't really written horror, but it can't be that big a jump from some of the science fiction you've done in the past. And who knows, if you give it a shot, you might be really good at it."

"Horror isn't really my thing," Owen began to explain, when he felt something stir and stretch at the base of his brain, scratching at it like a household pet scratches at a door. Horror wasn't a genre he was comfortable with, or at least it hadn't been, but images were playing in his brain, images of safe, tranquil places infiltrated by darkness and claimed by the monsters that lived there. He remembered a barn with a creek that ran behind it from his hometown. The barn belonged to a family friend who watched him after school. He wasn't supposed to play in the barn but no one could keep him away from it until the day he came across hundreds of hatching baby spiders. Yes. He could turn that into horror. It *was* horror. He hadn't had a trace of arachnophobia until that day, but that event changed him, turned him into the boot-wielding badass scourge of spider-kind he was today. Things changed once, they could change again. "Of course, my thing hasn't exactly been working out for me. It's worth a try. They haven't seen my work before."

"And on that note, I shall leave you," Christine said with a theatrical flourish as she rose from the couch. She pressed a kiss to his forehead and saw herself out, leaving him with his laptop.

He settled in for what he thought was going to be a session of staring at a blinking cursor on a blank page, but the second his fingers touched the keyboard they itched to type. Owen urged his fingers to be patient, to wait for the thoughts to form, but they already had, his fingers typing furiously to keep up.

***

Owen was dimly aware of the passage of time. Shadows cast by the mini blinds moved from one side of the room to the other and when the shadows disappeared the world outside had gone dark. His hand instinctively reached for the switch on the table lamp next to him. Though the light flicked on soft and yellow, Owen squinted and rubbed his eyes against its harshness. A half-remembered phrase tickled the back of his mind about darkness creeping in without notice. It was something he'd gleaned from a church sermon as a boy when he was much more apt to daydream and create his own stories than listen to parables, the morals of which were always slanted to serve the pastor's own end. He liked his own stories better. Still did.

Owen pushed the still-forming philosophical thoughts of darkness aside to focus on the darkness he hoped he'd created on the page.

First, he'd set the scene: the idyllic barn, so much like the one from his childhood, on a bright summer morning. He imagined that in a movie, the camera would zoom in on dewdrops, glistening crystals on a perfectly formed spider web. Then the lighting would dim so slightly as to barely be perceptible, but just enough to be the first unsettling hint that something wasn't right. Of course, he didn't have lighting tricks, just his words on the page. He made a few edits and read his first beat again. This time a shiver climbed the steps of his spine and greeted the thing that scratched at his brain and compelled him to write. He imagined the Compelling

Thing rolling like a spoiled housecat so that the Shiver might rub its tummy.

He counted beats as he read his narrative to make sure the pacing was right. If the story moved too fast he missed opportunities to build suspense, too slow and he bored the reader. Considering the somewhat cliché nature of the killer spider story, he knew the writing had to be perfect.

Through the eyes of the character, a younger, brighter-eyed version of himself, he saw a weathered, wooden door pulled open, groaning and creaking with every inch. Owen knew what was behind the door. For a fleeting second he considered deleting the next few paragraphs to spare this version of himself the fate he had written, but he wouldn't. This was horror and the character he had written was far too curious to walk away without knowing what caused that noise coming from behind the barn door. Only Owen knew that it was a newly awoken, giant spider demon clicking at the inside of the walls in search of a soft, warm place to lay her eggs, a place that would also serve as her spawn's first meal as they ate their way out of the nest and into the world. The door inched open.

Owen was just whispering goodbye to his first ever horror victim when a moving shadow caught the corner of his eye. He looked up from his computer, blinking to force his eyes to adjust, but when he focused on the wall there was nothing there. He scanned the room, looking for something that could have thrown the shape. By the angle of the light he reasoned that the only thing that could have cast a shadow in the proper direction was his own head, which didn't match.

He snorted his amusement. "You freaked yourself out, jackass," he said and then, rethinking his sentiment, added, "Cool."

As he returned his attention to his writing, he couldn't shake the desire to look over his shoulder. He continued to take it as a good sign and a motivator, which pleased the Compelling Thing rolling happily just under his skull.

It wasn't until the small hours of the morning, the sky outside turning from black to indigo, that the story was complete. The Compelling Thing took one final stretch before curling up and allowing Owen to do the same.

***

Owen's eyes darted to the clock at the lower right hand of his screen just as the time changed to 6:37. Christine was coming over at 7:00 with take-out, champagne, and her boyfriend, Brad. Owen and Christine celebrated a month prior when the contest winners were announced, his name glowing in the top three next to his story's title. However, Christine had just received her hard copy of the horror anthology and insisted that holding it in her hands and seeing "by Owen Porter" in print called for more celebration. He assumed celebrating also meant a good bit of congratulating herself for making him enter the contest to begin with, but it would be good to see her. He hadn't been around much since submitting his winning tale.

Immediately after the success of the spider story, he was inspired for another about a sinister stretch of highway. He was elated at how easily the story flowed, though unsure of where to submit it once complete. Then Owen received a message from the direct email address of one of the editors in charge of judging the contest. Impressed with that sort of attention, he opened it right away. The message congratulated him on his win, then said that the site was starting a new project that was half serial and half creature-feature. They wanted him to be a part of it as a regular paid gig with a small, but diverse, group of other writers. He replied with his acceptance and a draft of the haunted highway story.

Owen knew the drastic change between not having enough work to live and receiving multiple opportunities in the space of a couple weeks would take a toll, but he hadn't realized how far he'd let himself go until he looked in the mirror. Greasy hair gave way to scraggly sideburns and days-old stubble. A shave, a shower, and real clothes had been the first thing on the day's agenda.

He was tired. There had been many sleepless nights since he created his first monster and his eyes still chased shadows. He took it as a sign that he should rest, knowing that he wouldn't be able to, that he had to write until drained completely, or until the Compelling Thing was satisfied. The Compelling Thing was what worried him. Was Cat, as he had taken to calling it, simply what other writers meant when they said they wrote because they had to, that they'd go insane if they didn't, or was it something else? Cat certainly had a sadistic streak. One night, Owen slumped so low in his chair that he might has well have been on the floor, sobbing from exhaustion; still, Cat wouldn't let him rest. Cat scratched and yowled and poked him on through blurred vision and finger cramps. When rest finally came, Cat stalked Owen through his dreams. Owen reasoned, however, that lost sleep was a small price to pay to excel at job in which he didn't have to wear pants.

He pinched the fabric of his khakis between his fingers, one last irrational check to make sure he was wearing something other than sweats. This would be Owen's first time really hanging out with Brad, getting a chance to size him up. Making guilt-free assessments of Brad's character was a task that required real pants.

The knock on the door came a few minutes earlier than expected. Owen opened it to his guests.

Christine, in her standard jeans and tank top, threw her arms over her head in celebration. She had the anthology in one hand and a giant bottle of cheap champagne in the other. "Congratulations!" she declared in the semi-shrill voice that meant she was suppressing a squeal. Christine insisted that she didn't squeal unless a role called for it and went to great efforts to make sure that remained true. She kissed him on the cheek as she moved into his apartment.

Brad, in a khakis and t-shirt ensemble that mirrored Owen's own, carried in his left hand a large paper bag stapled closed at the top with a Chinese take-out menu attached. He held out a bottle of expensive bourbon with his right. Owen accepted the bottle with his left hand so he could offer his right for a proper, firm handshake.

"Thank you," Owen said as he took the obligatory look at the stately label on the bottle. "Kitchen's that way." He gestured in the direction Christine had gone.

"Cool," Brad replied and then added in a conspiratorial

tone before passing, "Don't tell Christine I said this, 'cause I'll deny it if you do, but your story scared the shit out of me."

"No worries. Secret's safe," Owen assured him, a puff of tension releasing itself in a laugh. "It's a huge compliment."

Within minutes they were enjoying themselves around the table, glasses full of champagne and mouths full of General Tso's chicken. Christine drained her glass in one swig, thirsty after making her common error of pouring too much soy sauce on her fried rice. "So," she began, locking eyes with Owen as she put her glass down, neglecting to refill it. "Write me a play."

"What?" Owen asked. He looked at Brad whose expression said he knew all about this turn of events. He looked back at Christine. "I mean, what do you mean, 'write you a play'?"

"I mean, you write a play and we'll put it up."

"You do understand what kind of stuff I'm writing right now, right?"

"Of course I do. Who's the one who got you to enter the contest to begin with?"

Owen knew she'd find a way to play that card tonight but this was more drastic than he'd imagined. He considered calling her on it when he felt what was becoming a familiar stir at the back of his mind, like something waking up. Cat's piqued attention silenced Owen as Christine continued. "People do successful fringe theatre all the time."

"It's true," Brad piped up. "With current technology and everyone having a device in their hands, niche type productions, and publications for that matter, have a chance to do incredibly well with the right promotion. It's actually an exciting time to be an artist."

"I know actors who'll do it, venues we can use, and I'm dating one of the best PR and marketing guys in the business," Christine said as she reached for Brad's hand.

"I don't know about all that but it is what I do for a living. This would just be way more interesting than the crap I usually have to promote."

It was clear to Owen that not only had Brad known about this in advance, but that Christine had carefully rehearsed it with him. "All we need is the playwright," she nudged.

The first thing Owen wanted to point out was that he had no experience as a playwright, but between the expectant looks of his guests, Cat pawing at the new prospect, and a certain degree of pleasure at the thought of writing specifically for Christine, he couldn't manage to voice the protest. The moment was broken by a buzzing in his pocket.

"You're not seriously going to answer that now?" Christine made her statement a question as Owen pulled out his cell phone.

Grateful for the interruption, Owen feigned an apologetic sigh. "It's my mom. You have to pick up for your mom." He answered, "Hi, Mom."

"Hi, honey," his mother's voice came through the phone. She sounded tired. "You've probably already heard—social media and all—but since I hadn't heard from you, I thought I'd call."

Every time Owen's mom called him with news from home, he reminded her about his internet connection and the tendencies of some to over-share online. Often times, he ended up filling in details for her. However, it wasn't uncommon for him to drop off of social media when he was deep into a project, and he was currently deep into many. "I actually haven't been online much lately," he confessed.

"That makes me feel better," she said and sighed. "Explains why you haven't called. Of course, now I have to be the one to tell you."

"Mom, what's going on?" Owen asked, grabbing his laptop and opening his social media sites. He gestured to Brad and Christine to wait a second, but their concerned looks told him they were just as anxious as he was.

"They found Emmie Snyder dead in the barn the other day."

Owen was just about to ask his mother if he'd heard her correctly when the computer screen confirmed that he had. Below the headline "Local Woman Found Dead," a photo of the Snyder family barn revealed just how well he'd recreated it in his tale, only now it was surrounded by yellow police tape.

"What happened?" Owen asked, scanning the article for details of which there were none and doing quick calculations in his head to try and guess at her age.

"No one is saying." his mom replied. "But by the way the police are swarming down there and keeping everyone else away, I think we can rule out natural causes."

"Oh shit." Owen said in a hoarse voice as he brought his hand to his mouth. Christine shifted in her seat and shot a worried glance at Brad.

"I hate to be the one to tell you but you hadn't called and Emmie had been so proud of you. She was just so tickled when I told her that her barn inspired the one in your story."

Owen felt Cat stir in his brain, just one indulgent roll before going still again. "I'm so sorry, Mom. Do you need anything? Does the family?"

"No, we're fine, and I actually have to go. Tonight's book club, and Emmie wouldn't have wanted us to skip it, bookish as she was."

"Okay, Mom. Please keep me posted," Owen said before they exchanged goodbyes and hung up. "Wow," he said.

"What's going on?" Christine asked.

He told Christine and Brad about his mother's half of the conversation. They responded with the expected condolences and questions of what they could do, which was absolutely nothing, before Owen insisted they all get back to enjoying dinner. He heard very little of what they were saying anyway. In his head, he was already brainstorming the play he hadn't yet agreed to write. Cat purred.

***

Owen slammed his elbows on the table and dropped his head in his hands. "I'm losing my fucking mind," he muttered before ripping his fingers through his hair. He lifted his head and pleaded with the air. "How much more blood do I have to give you?"

Cat continued its relentless scratching.

Owen thought he was writing a tongue-in-cheek type of horror story about a shape shifting demon that survived by emulating other supernatural creatures. He'd expected writing it to be fun, to have a chance to play around with classic horror tropes without retelling the same old monster stories. Once he started writing, that all changed.

It wasn't enough for the demon in the guise of a vampire to seduce and drink a victim into a prune; there had to be torture and humiliation such that when the scene finally ended in a spray of blood, he slumped over, limp with the relief that he didn't have to write it anymore. It wasn't enough for the demon's werewolf incarnation to rip its prey apart. Owen had to describe in long, agonizing detail the way slick entrails gleam and steam in moonlight. Each time he manifested his demon he threw more blood at the page. The more blood he wrote, the more blood he had to write to satisfy Cat.

It was while writing the demon as a particularly vicious swamp creature, one with intentions too deviant and horrid for Owen to write for his beautiful young victim, that he decided he simply wouldn't. He had thought, as he closed his laptop, that he would get some sleep and pick it up again with a clearer head later.

Having worked himself into exhaustion too deep to

bother to get to the bedroom, he reclined on the couch and pulled a fleece blanket over himself. Owen whispered a relaxation mantra, closed his eyes, and inhaled deeply. He had barely exhaled when a bright light pierced the eyes-closed darkness. The light brought with it a headache that felt as though something were very literally scratching at Owen's brain. He knew—as he released a scream he'd never heard from anything human, let alone himself—that something was. He had no choice but to get back to work and once he did, the pain melted.

"I'm losing my fucking mind," he said and believed it. Normal people didn't become this obsessed with a project. Healthy people didn't get skull-crushing headaches when they tried to stop working. Sane people didn't entertain for even a fleeting moment that perhaps a condition like his was less a matter of obsession than possession, and they certainly didn't believe in entities that took residence in their brains and compelled them to create things. Owen did.

He believed it more and more as he kept his fingertips moving across the keyboard, afraid of what would happen if he paused to rub his eyes or take a drink of water. He had a very clear vision of himself typing until the flesh of his fingers wore away and exposed bone was all that was left to click at the keys. He watched his skeletal self continue to type in spite of cramping in muscles that were no longer there. He had become his own horror story.

His story wasn't the one forcing its way through his mind and materializing on the page. He wondered though, as he wrote the swamp demon bearing down on the young man who knew what was coming because he'd just seen it happen, if the next death he would write—would need to write—would be his own.

***

Owen sat in the café and did his best to appear alert and at ease. He knew he failed as he leaned and bobbed to align himself with a mirrored beer plaque on the wall. His reflection confirmed his suspicion. The dimmed lights did little to hide the bags under his eyes and he didn't need the mirror to see how he'd shredded the label on his beer bottle. He took a deep breath, swallowed his anxiety, and did his best to perk up. It would do no good for Christine to spend the entire meeting fretting over what was wrong with him.

He was meeting Christine and Brad to talk about the play and he was early. Cat saw to that with its poking and nudging. Owen discovered it was best to oblige Cat in the prodding stage. However, Cat hadn't calmed much. It was like it was on edge, crouched and waiting on pins to attack. "I'm losing my fucking mind," Owen whispered to himself. He looked up and saw the female server who had been on her way to over to him change course. A male server came to ask him if he needed anything. Owen ordered a beer and asked the server for three menus. On his return, the server looked inappropriately relieved to see Brad and Christine walk in and wave a greeting to Owen. Did he look that bad?

The look on Christine's face confirmed that he did. "Good goddess, Owen! You look like a big bowl of crap salad."

"And you're looking lovely as ever this evening," Owen replied dryly and looked past her. "Hi Brad," he said with a nod.

"Hey," Brad said, returning the gesture. "Seriously though, when was the last time you slept?"

"Or ate?" Christine added.

Owen suspected his clothes had been fitting more loosely lately, but it was the last worry on his mind. "You know how I get."

"Yes," Christine answered. "I know how you get when you're on a depression fueled drug bender. You're not on a depression fueled drug bender are you?"

"No, I'm not," Owen assured her while simultaneously

wishing that actually was what was wrong with him. "I'm living the writer's dream." He silently acknowledged that technically, nightmares were dreams too. "The muses are being incredibly generous with the inspiration and people want to buy what I create. Sometimes that means I work too long and forget to eat, but I'm okay."

Owen could tell Christine didn't believe him, and thus Brad didn't believe him either, but neither of them questioned him as the server approached. After a recitation of the specials and the polite small talk, Christine proceeded to order every other deep fried appetizer on the menu and a pitcher of the heaviest beer on tap.

Owen leaned in to whisper to Christine. "You can't put all my weight back on me in one night."

"Doesn't mean I can't try." She smiled and squeezed his knee. Brad didn't notice. "So, about the play," Christine changed the subject.

"About the play," Owen leaned in to the table and did his best to prove his words about being okay were true. "I've actually come up with outlines for three very short plays that each have an urban legend type of feel. I can tie them together, like each play is being told at a sleepover or around a campfire."

Christine nodded. "This could work…" she started to

say before letting her thought trail off without her words.

Owen picked up where she left off. "It works mainly because it can be done with varying cast sizes. Each role can be cast with a different actor for a large cast or we can double, even triple up some roles with a smaller one."

"I have six actors who say they are definitely in," Christine said. "Plus me, that's lucky number seven."

"And these six actors are as informed as you are about what I write?" Owen asked.

"Gave them all links to your work. It mostly made them more excited." Christine barely took a breath before moving on. "Now, until the work is done and the thing is cast, we can expect a couple of people to drop out and a couple more to be interested, but we're prepared for that. However, we also need to consider that our venue will most likely be very small."

"Okay," Owen said with a genuine smile. He knew Christine was just getting started. "Small venue."

"Oh, but that shouldn't limit you!" Christine exclaimed and rattled on as the food arrived.

Owen, caught up in Christine's excitement and planning, had almost forgotten about his fears and the torture that writing had become as he shoveled onion rings into his mouth and washed them down with a thick, flavorful stout.

His cramped fingers had stretched out to give Brad a number of high fives. His face had produced every smile it could to reassure Christine, most pointedly when she mused over whether she could direct and act in the same show. Things were almost good, but as he looked up to call the server and order shots, a headline on the television above the bar caught his attention.

"What would you like to drink?" the server asked.

"Can you have the bartender turn the TV up or turn on the closed captioning?" Owen asked, no longer interested in the tequila that would have made his mouth water seconds ago.

"Owen, what's wrong?" he heard Christine ask but couldn't register the meaning.

The headline on the screen said, "Hell Highway Claims Sixth."

"Sensational headline," Brad muttered.

What Owen could take from muffled sound, poor captioning, and much poorer lip reading on his part, was that in the past month there had been six different accidents, each involving a single driver, each on the same stretch of highway. The news report cut to footage of an accident scene and Owen's breath caught in his chest. He recognized it all as if it had been plucked from his own mind's eye and was not surprised when the caption said that investigations had not turned up a cause.

This story was followed by one of a grisly attack of a young couple on protected wetlands. Local police had yet to figure out what kind of creature could have reduced the bodies to piles of bloody parts. The report cut to a video clip of a police officer vomiting on the scene.

A third story showed Owen a familiar street in his hometown with a headline he couldn't bring himself to read. He already knew what it said.

Owen also knew what was causing the accidents on that stretch of highway. He knew what killed the teenagers in the wetland, how it was connected to the bloodless corpse three miles away, and why the authorities wouldn't make the connection before it killed again. As much as it pained him to think it and as much as he hoped he was wrong, he knew what killed Emmie Snyder.

"I'm losing my fucking mind," Owen whispered the words that had become a mantra. He felt every fried thing he ate try to crawl back up his throat. "I have to go," he said out loud and stood up.

"Owen, no," Christine argued. "You're white as a sheet."

"And talking about losing your mind," Brad added.

"I have to go," he repeated. "Don't worry. I've got the play under control. I just have to go." He walked away, ignoring the sound of their protest behind him.

***

Owen closed and locked the door behind him, throwing himself against it as though he could keep the world out, as though what he was afraid of wasn't already inside. He dialed his mother. Although he'd already jumped to conclusions, he needed the validation that the conclusions were right. He had to know that maybe, just maybe, he wasn't really going mad.

"Pick up. Pick UP!" he yelled at the phone.

"Hello," his mother's voice finally answered.

"Hi, Mom," Owen said. At the sound of his mother's voice, he lost some of his resolve to prove to himself he was sane. He knew that being sane meant he killed Emmie, or at least created the thing that did. It was precisely why he had to know. He wet his lips and swallowed hard. "Listen, I have something to ask you, and I need you to be straight with me no matter how strange you think it is."

"Of course," she replied. "Honey, are you okay?"

Owen couldn't answer the question honestly so he

pretended he hadn't heard it. "Outside of what the news is saying about Emmie's death, what's being said around town?" The phone was silent. "Mom?"

"Yes. I'm still here." Another eternal second of silence passed. "It's just damn strange as hell."

"That's why I said what I said."

"Yeah, well, to a degree, it's typical. Cops keep a tight lock on the place and don't say a thing, so no one knows a thing. Everyone speculates and every tidbit of information that does leak leads to more speculation and wild stories."

"Uh huh," Owen said, making a get-on-with-it motion with his free hand that he would never make if face to face with his mother.

"It's just that this time what they're saying, I mean, for the love of Saint Fuck!" Blasphemy from his mother was never a good sign. As a church-going woman, she might curse until a vein popped out of her neck but blasphemy wasn't generally part of her repertoire.

"Mom," Owen said, trying to keep his voice from shaking. "What are they saying?"

"They're saying, I mean, it's not that weird for a body to have bug eggs in it. Insects lay eggs in exposed corpses all the time. But there's been a whisper or two that the rest of her insides were…" Owen's mother took a quavering breath.

Owen could almost hear her shudder.

He finished the sentence his mother couldn't. "Liquefied." *Like what a spider demon the size of an SUV venomously does to its prey before laying its eggs inside,* was the part he didn't say.

"Yes, liquefied," she said with a certain conviction, as if hearing it had given her the courage to say it. "They're saying her internal organs were fucking liquefied! I might have known a gruesome detail like that would have found its way online." His mother was dangerously approaching a rant when she shifted to fighting tears. "Emmie deserved better than these sick stories shared for internet *entertainment.*" She spat the last word.

Owen wanted to defend the internet and admit that he hadn't seen it online, but had no idea what to tell her when she inevitably asked how he'd known. How could he tell her that he knew what people were saying about the death of a dear family friend because he'd written the tale they were telling? "Mom, I have to go. Thank you for clearing this all up," he said, although the sick feeling in his stomach rolled with a searing intensity that made Cat look like an amateur. He'd killed Emmie.

"Okay, honey," his mother replied without argument. Owen suspected she wanted to collect herself. "Are you sure you're okay?" she asked, forgetting he hadn't answered her the first time she'd asked.

"Yes." *No.* It occurred to Owen he had to warn his mother, though he had no idea what to say. "Mom?"

"Yes."

"Just, I don't know. When you're out, and even at home, be careful, okay? The news in general is getting weird lately."

"Of course. I'm always careful. Honey, are you—"

"I love you, Mom." He cut her off and hung up.

He managed to get to the kitchen sink before he threw up. Head and shoulders bent as he heaved, he turned on the faucet and flipped a switch. The garbage disposal came on with a whirring gurgle that kept Owen focused. Grateful he'd done his dishes, he pulled the hose out of its hole in the stainless steel and aimed the sprayer at the lingering vomit. It was a mess he could clean and the act of doing it calmed him. Maybe he could clean some of his other messes too.

He was done writing; there was no question about that, and there had to be something he could do about the work he already had out. A part of him knew ridding the world of his spider demon would be impossible. It was out in the world— both in hard copy and online—attached to money he didn't control. Owen doubted the work he'd written solely for the website where he might have some clout stood a better chance of removal. It didn't really matter. It was common knowledge that once something went on the internet, it never really went away. "But I still have to try," he said out loud. "First, I'll have to break it to Christine. No play." He started talking himself through the action he was going take as he opened his laptop, but didn't sit. Motion was necessary. "Then I need to try and convince the magazine to pull my contributions."

"I wouldn't do that," a voice interrupted him.

Owen snapped his head up at the sound of the intruder, asking himself where he'd come from and how he'd gotten in. Then the man's appearance registered, the casually expensive clothing and the dark hair styled neatly around angular features. Owen felt phantom heat in his hand the instant his eyes made contact with the unnaturally green ones. "You," he said and cringed the second the word left his mouth. Had he written it, he would have deleted it immediately.

Perhaps as a bit of mercy, his intruder rolled past his cliché response. "It will make you appear painfully stupid and won't make any difference for your trouble," he said.

"I killed those people," Owen said.

The man laughed, an elegant sound that still filled the

room as if it were coming from the air and not his mouth. "Is that what you're worried about?" He broke for more laughter. "Well, then this is easy enough to solve. You didn't kill anyone."

Owen had no intention of arguing semantics. "Fine. I didn't kill anyone, but I created the monsters that did."

"Is that what you think?" he asked, taking a step toward Owen. Owen straightened his spine but would not step back. "You didn't create anything, Owen Porter. You're just the doorway." He tapped the top of Owen's head in a condescending manner and turned his back to him. He strode to the couch and sat on the arm in a casual pose, legs stretched and arms crossed in front of him. "Truth is, you're not that good, but my children needed to be brought to life here somehow. You may not be the strongest portal I've ever used, but that's what you are and I'm grateful to you for your service."

"You're welcome," he said, followed by an indignant, "I'm done."

"Oh, but you're not," he said. "You've made a deal with a demon and I've kept up my end of the bargain. You have a lovely apartment that you've been able to continue living in, your bills are paid, and you did it all by writing stories. Not a customer service job in sight. The deal stands, and you will keep up your end of it."

"You tricked me into making a deal." Owen fought to keep his voice strong.

"Of course I did," the demon said with a shrug. "And that changes absolutely squat. We demons wouldn't get very far if we went around being honest about what we are. Hell, it was a bunch of writers who made sure of that." He narrowed his eyes. "And we are well past the days when people who know what we are come to literal crossroads looking for us.

"Yes, I tricked you. I tricked you while you were tripping balls, desperate in a corner at a party, at a crossroads in your life. Look at you now. That scenario could have ended a lot worse if you ask me."

"I didn't ask you, and you can't force me to write."

"I truly hoped it wouldn't come to this with you, Owen," the demon said without moving.

Owen opened his mouth to ask what the demon meant but couldn't squeak out a sound before pain exploded in his head, knocking him to the floor. He squinted through the torment at the demon who only smirked. Cat awoke and tore at his mind like a long lost scratching post as his newest inspiration came.

Owen couldn't get enough of a handle on the monster to

describe it, and he soon realized it was because his mind's eye was writing it from the monster's point of view. Hungry for both sustenance and violence, it stalked its preferred prey, which Owen knew to be tall, willowy brunettes with nice singing voices, the kind of voices perfect for the theatre. The words forming in his head described the sound of a shower running accompanied by a woman's lyrical voice. The voice was familiar. The monster turned a corner to a steaming bathroom that Owen immediately recognized as Christine's. "No," he said to the demon whose smirk grew into a grin. That grin superimposed itself over the explicit and brutal scene of Christine's murder. "No!" Owen cried, and pressed his forehead to the floor.

The demon rose from the couch and moved toward Owen. He placed a finger under Owen's chin, raising it to force eye contact. "If you don't want to write like a good little boy, then I'll have to force you to write, and this is the story I will force. Do you want that?"

"No," Owen said. He didn't voice his questions about whether or not the demon could really make that happen. It wasn't worth the chance. "What do I need to do?"

"The same as you always needed to do," the demon shrugged and gave a reassuring smile. "Just write. Finish the play. Christine will be safe and she'll play all the best roles because you wrote them for her. Should the time come that my little ingénue-eating monster needs to be born, well, we'll make sure he has a taste for red heads." He chuckled and the sound rolled Owen's stomach. "Will that work for you?"

"Yes." It wouldn't, but there was nothing he could do about it in the moment. He needed time and he needed sleep. "May I make an addendum to my deal?"

"You may propose one."

"I assume that tricking me into a deal you won't let me out of means that you need me. Is that so?"

"In a way," the demon replied. "It would be *inconvenient* for me to lose you."

"Then acknowledge that I'm human, that in order to create any percentage of these stories I need fundamental things like food and sleep. I'll do as you ask, but call your children off of scratching at my brain door every now and then."

"This is an addendum to which I'll agree," the demon said and put out his hand. Owen braced himself and offered his hand in return. "No seal this time," the demon said as he took Owens hand. "This is just an addendum."

They shook hands and Owen was alone.

***

Owen smiled. The play would be finished before the end of the page. While his demon sponsor had honored the addendum to their agreement, granting him time for his human needs, the reality of what was happening and his role in it rendered him barely able to eat or sleep. He went through all the motions though, insisting on taking his time and forcing the demon and his monsters to honor a schedule. Still, Owen was pleased that it was coming to a close.

It hurt him to lie to Christine the way he had been for the past couple of weeks. He couldn't stand watching her eyes light up when they talked about the play like it was actually going to happen. He hated pretending everything was normal when all he wanted to do was warn her, but his very simple plan depended on following the demon's plan.

Owen was down to his final line and stage direction. "Almost time to celebrate," he said out loud as he pushed himself away from the table. He poured himself a glass of bourbon, took a drink, and placed the glass and the bottle both on the table next to a pack of cigarettes as he passed into the hall. He pulled an ornate, hand carved box from the hall closet and brought it back to the table with him. The box was the last piece of the puzzle and had been easy to acquire.

Owen had managed to look healthy enough on a visit to his mother—she'd been so sad since Emmie died—that she didn't question his sudden interest in his grandfather's gun. "He's smiling down on you, knowing that you finally want this," she said proudly. As she handed him the box, she added, "Having it doesn't mean you have to fire it." Emmie's passing had renewed his mother's reverence for the wishes of the dead, and it wasn't as though she was being left unarmed. Owen's father hunted and there were a couple of working rifles on the property.

He stroked the intricate carving and unlocked the box. Owen himself knew very little about guns, but he knew that what gleamed back at him was a .44 Magnum. His grandfather had told him so, and according to a Clint Eastwood flick he'd watched with Granddad as a kid, it could blow a man's head clean off. He hoped it could do the same to a demon.

Horror isn't really my thing. The words he'd said to Christine echoed like a taunt in his head. If horror had been more his thing, he might have formulated a plan that rested on more than a thin hope that it would work, but he had to be confident that beheading would do it. Nothing functioned without a head, and the Magnum was his best shot at separating the demon from his.

With his booze, smokes, and gun all together, he typed the final words of his horror play. He tapped a couple of keys and the printer across the room came to life, spitting out the first and last hard copy of the last thing he would ever write. Customer service looked pretty good after all of this. Maybe an office job would suit him a bit better now.

He lit a cigarette and followed his first drag with a sip of bourbon that he rolled around his tongue, really tasting it. He took another drag from his cigarette and exhaled slowly, watching patterns form and fall apart in the wisps of smoke. Then another sip of bourbon. He repeated the pattern until the cigarette burned to the filter. "Showtime," he said as he tucked the Magnum into his pants and took the pages from the printer. Positioning his portable paper shredder at the best possible vantage point, he began summoning the demon the only way he knew how.

The shredder whirred to life as Owen fed it the first page of the play, followed by the second. Slowly, he fed the third page and on. Prepared to print the play again and start over if he had to, he kept feeding pages through the machine's jaws.

"I told you that would do you no good," the demon said as he materialized from the hallway and added, "you idiot."

"I know. I'm just a portal and a very raw part of my

brain tells me the monsters have already come through." Owen felt the gun in his waistband pressing against him. He had to do this now. Hesitation for any reason, fear, uncertainty, or especially a grand speech, stood a strong chance of getting him killed. "I just needed to get you here," he said as he drew the gun, pointed, and fired. Although he'd braced for the recoil, it knocked him off balance and it took him a second to regain his footing. When he did, he saw the demon's body on the floor, head still attached. Owen, having no faith in his marksmanship, suspected he would need a second shot and strode to the body, gun out and pointed at the base of its neck. Something black and sticky was beginning to pool there. Just as he was about to take his second shot, the body vanished.

"That only works on humans possessed by demons, you fucking moron!" the demon's voice boomed. Owen spun and saw that the demon had materialized unscathed on the other side of the room. "And you're about to wish you'd never attempted that move."

Owen felt the stirring in his brain, the stirring that he knew was going to lead to the shattering pain of evil trying to break through his skull and into the world. He knew which monster would lead the charge. The words describing Christine's murder were doing an eloquent dance in his pounding head. The images made him want to gouge his mind's eye out.

In that moment, he knew how his final scene was going to play out. He knew how he was going to keep Christine safe. He knew how to make sure that no more monsters made it into the world and how to ensure that he would never be used like this again. *You're just a portal*, the words that once stung him gave him strength in his final act. "I'm just a portal," he said through clenched teeth as he raised the gun to his own head and aimed it at the door within. "Time to destroy it."

"NO!" The demon's scream was the last thing Owen heard before he pulled the trigger, sending a bullet ripping through his brain.

***

Christine walked out for curtain call to applause that seemed too loud for the venue. Although she'd performed to bigger houses, this was by far the most adoration she'd received on stage. She allowed a couple bittersweet tears to roll down her cheeks. She wished Owen was alive to see his final project come to fruition, and to see that so many people loved it. She thought of how proud he would be to see the house full again and again, and wondered if it would have been enough to stop him from taking his life.

She'd known that he was getting obsessive about the work. He'd admitted to sometimes forgetting to eat, or losing track of how long it had been since he'd last slept, but she'd never once thought he was in that dark a place.

She guessed people never did, though that thought neither alleviated her guilt nor helped her feel his loss any less. "There has to be a better way to honor him," Christine whispered to Brad at the memorial service. "He hated this stuff."

"I think I might have a better idea," came a voice from behind them. Christine knew immediately that the man was one of Owen's business associates. He didn't look bereaved enough be family, and he was too clean-cut to be one of Owen's friends. He went on to tell them that he was, indeed, an associate of Owen's and that Owen had spoken to him about the play. He had the finished copy.

"What do you need me to do?" Christine had asked eagerly. She wanted more than anything to honor Owen by bringing his final piece to life.

The man grinned so wide it reached his flashing green eyes. "Just act," he said. "All I need you to do is act."

ABOUT THE AUTHOR

Devon L. Miller currently resides in the greater Seattle area with her husband and their little black cat. When she's not writing, she can be found tempting fate on volcanoes or working one day job or another.

devonlmiller.com

Made in the USA
San Bernardino, CA
29 September 2015